The Girl In The Well

CECIL FREEMAN BEELER

THE PUBLISHERS
Red Deer College Press
56 Avenue & 32 Street Box 5005
Red Deer Alberta Canada T4N 5H5

CREDITS
Cover Art by Yvette Moore
Cover design by Jim Brennan
Text design by Dennis Johnson
Printed & bound in Canada by Gagné Printing Ltée

ACKNOWLEDGMENTS
The Publishers gratefully acknowledge the financial contribution of the Alberta Foundation for the Arts, Alberta Culture & Multiculturalism, the Canada Council, Red Deer College & Radio 7 CKRD.
Special thanks to Carolyn Dearden, David More and Clark Daniels for their assistance in preparation of this book.

CANADIAN CATALOGUING IN PUBLICATION DATA
Beeler, Cecil Freeman, 1915–
The girl in the well
ISBN 0-88995-075-X
I. Title II. Author
PS8553.E34G5 1991 JC813'.54 C91-091220-3
PZ7.B44GI 1991

CONTENTS

CHAPTER 1

Girl in the Well

"Hello-woe-woe," I yelled to the girl down in the well. "My name is Corinne Kragh. Who are you-woo-woo?"

My big old horse, Moses, black except for his three chestnut stockings, pointed his ears at the hollow, whoomy sounds in the well.

I was leaning on the square top of the well with my head in the round hole. My yelling echoed back nice and loud because the well in the winter was almost empty.

"I can see you," I called, "but I can't see who you are."

I saw her head between a pair of yellow leather mitts like mine and against a circle of bright blue sky. She had on a toque and a brown scarf, too, but I couldn't see the rest of her. I turned my head a little and the cold sun lit her face.

"Oh, now I see you."

Moses snorted and banged the wooden trough with his hoof, but I wasn't through yet.

"Why isn't your face roundy-round like all the other kids. Look at that cheek – flat as a pancake. No wonder teacher said a face like that looks old enough for the mama's part in the school play."

Moses snorted some more. He stepped back a little, crunching the snow under his hooves. Every step in the cold snow crackled like six. I stepped away expecting he would lean across the water trough to poke me with his nose. That's how he always tells me he's waiting for his drink.

"It must be great to live down there," I told the girl in the well. "No dishes to wash, no firewood to chop and no mean old horse – Moses, quit banging around like that – to fill up with water. And mostly, no Mertie Henshaw sneaking around to make a fight just when you don't expect him."

I pulled my head up and looked toward the two big willow trees at the gate, where anybody would come from the Henshaw's place, for a boy in a green and brown mackinaw jacket with rabbit snares in his button hole.

"I wish I could live down there, too," I whispered to the girl in the well. A teardrop splatted into the water and made wrinkles on her face. "I bet you even have a daddy."

The horse whickered loudly.

"Can't you wait just a minute, Moses?" I lifted my face out of the well again. "You know I'm going to – "

Going to bump into a dirty old dead rabbit stuck in my face, as it turned out. Mertie Henshaw thinks it's cute to sneak up behind me and do something to get me mad.

"You rabbit!" I scolded.

"Nope," said Mertie in that squawky voice of his. He shoved the carcass at me, then back so I couldn't grab it. "It's a jack rabbit. Can't you tell the difference?"

I spit out rabbit hairs – jack rabbit hairs, all right – and tried to grab Mertie's hand. He held it behind his back.

"This beauty from the prairies is twice as big as our bush rabbits." He turned the white-furred carcass around in his hands. "With some potatoes and turnips he's plenty for a dinner."

"You're a sneaking bush rabbit!" I snarled at him. Mertie hated to be called that.

"Yeah? Who do you say has buck teeth and long ears? Come on, say it." He held the rabbit like a ball bat, ready to hit me.

"A pig doesn't," I said.

He clumped me on the head.

"Take that back," he said.

"Bush rabbit!" I yelled.

He hit me harder, but I grinned at him.

"Take it all back," Mertie screamed.

"You stop pounding me," I said, "before I get good and mad."

"Go ahead – get mad." He banged me with the rabbit until its legs broke. He looked at it, and he looked at me.

"You get out of here right now," I scowled at him. "Go home before I – "

"Yeah? What if I don't?" Mertie wobbled the rabbit at me, but he backed up a few steps. "Would you run in to your ma?"

I gave him my yellow leather mitt, with a fist curled up in it, right in the chops.

Mertie stood grinning that mean little three-cornered grin of his.

"Your dad can't do nothing for you since he ran away."

When I was just little, Karl used to scowl Mertie away if he got too mean to me. When I got bigger I took my own part with a lot of boxing tricks I learned roughhousing with Karl.

"He did not run away," I said, some of it to myself.

"If he didn't," said Mertie, "why isn't he sticking around?"

"Was he supposed to ask you if he could go some place?"

"Did a policeman catch him bootlegging, or did they take him away to the crazy house?"

This time Mertie got both my fists, hard as hammers, and he got them two or three times around. He dropped his rabbit and hopped to the other side of the well where I couldn't reach him.

"My fist is harder than a frozen old rabbit, eh?" I said.

Mertie just blinked, twitched his nose a time or two, then hopped through the deep snow toward the big willows. He didn't bother about any old rabbit, and I didn't either. He would sneak back for it after dark.

"Hello, Me – " I said into the well. That's as far as I could go for a while because I sobbed a little, something like hiccups.

"I never know the best way to do anything until I go ahead and do it all wrong."

I didn't mean Mertie at all. The girl in the well knew that, too. She got wrinkles in rings, like tears or something were falling in the water. I wasn't crying – just trying not to.

Moses snorted real mad at me and banged the trough hard.

"One more second, Moses." I reached out my hand toward the pail, which didn't fool him one bit. I had one last word to send down the well.

"Who is the meanest meanie, Mertie or Karl?" I asked.

I took the well pail and a coiled rope tied to it from its tree branch and let it go easy down the well.

"Or maybe it's me," I said to the girl in the well.

The pail splashed into the water, and Me was gone in a bunch of wrinkles. I wanted to tell her all about it, but it was too late now.

I dragged the filled pail up from the well and staggered with it the few steps to the water trough. The trough was filled with a solid block of ice except for a small hollowed-out place like a bowl. I poured the water there, and Moses dipped his chin in it. He sucked it empty before I could hurry another pailful to him. Pail after pail went into the trough and right away out again.

"Moses!" I scolded, looking at the water gurgling away in his neck. "You got to leave some water in the well for the wood-haulers when they come."

At last he lifted his head, champing his teeth from the freezing water. He shivered, too, from so much of it in him.

"Great," I said. "You're filled up at last."

I slid the cover over the well and a sack of straw on top of that to keep the winter's cold out. I climbed on the water trough and rolled onto the horse's back. "Gitup, Moses."

Moses' hooves crunched along toward the log stable. I lay along his back, my nose in his mane, which felt at least partly warm.

"You tried to tell me about Mertie sneaking around with that dirty old rabbit, didn't you, Moses? You told me real loud, but I didn't listen to you."

Moses snorted steamy clouds around his head.

"Oh, Moses!" My arms went down around his neck and hugged him real tight. "Karl wouldn't listen to me when he wanted to go away. Then that terrible beating – oh!"

My tears were freezing in the horse's mane.

"You're the only friend I have to talk with, Moses. You and Pokie."

CHAPTER 2

THESE PICTURES

Some of our wood-haulers came while I was in the stable looking after Moses, then some more while I was doing the chickens. They threw off their hay or oat sheaves by the stable, and then they drove out to the bush to load up their sleighs with firewood poles before dark set in. When I came in the house, their bed rolls and grub boxes were everywhere around the kitchen floor.

"Come, my Karenne," said Mama, comb and hairbrush in her hand.

"Mama, what do you want me for?" I asked. "When you say 'Corinne' in the Old Country way, I know it's something."

"I make you nice the little girl for the wood-haulers."

"Why do I have to look nice for them, Mama?"

"The old coat is so much dusty," she said. I pulled off my work coat, which had been cut from Mama's old coat. "The overalls – is here a girl?"

"How can I wear something fancy if I look after Moses and the chickens and stuff?" I slipped off the strap overalls that made Karl call me his top hired hand. "I got to keep on my gum boots for the cold floor, Mama."

"You keep," said Mama. "Here. This make you the nice girl to see." She pulled a dress printed with flowers like summer over my jumbo knit sweater and felt trousers. A bit of the sweater poked out of a sleeve.

"This is good enough," I told her. "I don't want them to look at me anyway."

"Tish!" said Mama, pulling me between her knees and brushing down my hair until it was as firm and smooth as a bread loaf and about the same brown color. "You make nice with people. Not make shy with the stranger, not make fight with the nice little boy."

"Mertie Henshaw? A nice little boy? You should see him in school."

From Mama's flying fingers came two flat braids that started each side of the back of my head, circled around my forehead and went on toward the back. I'd die if I had to go to school in braids. Mertie would yank my head off my neck.

Every so often Mama wanted to make me look more like a girl. Mertie wanted to make me act like a girl all the time and tried to pound me down to size when I was bigger'n smarter'n him.

"No school now," said Mama. Her fingers felt great in my hair. "Just for me I make pretty Old Country girl."

The winter was so cold in 1934 the school closed down all January so kids wouldn't freeze to death trying to go. Only the wood-haulers came from the prairies to buy wood from us, or they would freeze.

I used to wonder why the wood-haulers didn't chop their own trees for firewood instead of buying some from us.

"Is on the prairies," Mama told me once. "One tree does not grow for miles and miles."

No trees? Wasn't that something! What if we lived on the prairies, I wondered. Darned old bush that I had lived in all my life – can't see anywhere for all the trees. The wood-haulers, the mean ones, called us bush rabbits.

Mama's fingers felt ticklish and nice in my hair.

"Go now." She finished with a little spank of the hair brush. "You make hot the stove to cook the wood-haulers."

"Mama." I wrinkled my nose. "Sometimes it doesn't come out right when you talk English like Old Country."

I went through the door from the sleeping part into the kitchen part of our log house. Two wood-haulers had come in while Mama did my hair and stood at the black kitchen stove frying slices of beef and potatoes. Two more sat at the table eating what they had cooked. Another was shaking out his blanket roll on the floor.

I looked around and at first couldn't see my little stool Karl made when I was just a tiny thing. Then I found a kid, a year or two older'n me, squatting on it with his knees up to his chin and rolling his eyes my way. I couldn't use it myself any more, but I didn't want a big lumpus like that sitting on my stool.

We had only four chairs. When we had more wood-haulers than that they sat on their grub boxes. This kid was trying to make me mad. Mertie and wood-haulers were just the same. I sat on the woodbin and tried to swallow some of the mad I felt.

"Lookee, Dad," he said. "It isn't even big enough for a prairie gopher to sit on."

I stood up again, ready to smash him even if he was a wood-hauler, and we needed the money.

"No good, though. Look how it wobbles." He wiggled the stool on its legs until they just about came off.

I picked up a stick of firewood in my hand.

"Sammy, behave yourself," said one of the men, looking at me, not Sammy. "You're a big boy now."

"Aw, Dad, just a little fun." Sammy got off my stool, grinning.

I put the firewood in the stove and sat down again, looking hard at the wall in front of me. Instead of the logs and dried mud, I was really looking at a picture of Mama and Karl and a wriggly giggling little Corinne above his head, tossed up in those big hands of his.

"Oh, Karl," I am laughing and kicking my legs. "Now I'm bigger'n all of you."

That was always my first picture, and it really happened a

long time ago.

The wood-haulers talked and laughed among themselves. Mama was in the other room softly singing an Old Country song to herself. Nobody but me could see my picture anyway.

Mama couldn't sing the tickley little runs and trills in the music that sounded so great when she played her little red accordion. But I could put them into my picture, accordion and all.

Karl has let me down from my first picture, and now I'm sitting on the floor under the accordion. Mama is playing a kicking polka, her fingers popping the white buttons in and out. Karl pulls me up by the hands, and we do the Old Country dance that is mostly kicking. When we can't dance any more from laughing so hard, Karl finishes by tossing me above his head.

Mama said we were more like two kids together than a father and his little girl.

Now Karl was gone, the red accordion was packed away under Mama's bed, and nothing was like it once was.

Mama was making our supper on our little tin heater. The smell of chicken stew drifted through the partition almost as strong as the rich smell of the steaks sizzling on the stove. When I stood up to push another stick of firewood into the stove, something fell from the neck of my dress and swung *plok* against the woodbin.

I screamed inside myself, "Oh, my pendant, my pendant!" I picked it up by its chain and held it on the flat of my hand. The gold back wasn't scratched. The sides weren't dented either. I turned it over. The glass face wasn't broken or loosened, and the two golden 'K's' tangled together on the black backing were just the same as always.

Great luck, the pendant wasn't hurt at all. I tucked it away with a special pat to tell it not to fall out any more.

"That ain't yours," Mertie had said in one of his almost

nice talks with me. "Them 'K's' stand for Karl Kragh."

"No they don't. It was always mine."

"Ah, ha. Then you spell both your names with a 'K'?"

"Smarty. They really stand for Karl and Karen, my Mama. They brought this pendant from the Old Country to give it to me as soon as I was born."

"By the yiping piping – " One of the wood-haulers clawed around deep in his grub box. What was the matter – oh, I knew. My loose boots went *sklumf, sklumf* across the floor as I went to our cupboard, then back to the man with salt and pepper shakers held out on the flat of my hand.

I kept my face turned down and a little to the side. These noisy prairie people liked to tease and tease and tease until they could laugh at somebody.

"Tha-anks so much," the man said, surprised. "How did you know I forgot these important items?"

He shook the salt and pepper around his plate, one shaker in each hand.

"Much appreciated," he said, handing them back. "You're a very considerate young lady."

I looked up into his grinning brown eyes. Nobody said anything like that to me, ever, and he meant it nice and not a bit smarty. I couldn't help a tiny smile as I hurried back to the woodbin even though my ears felt red.

". . . horse got a bad cut, and I just couldn't stop the bleeding." The wood-haulers were talking among themselves. "Finally packed the cut with flour and put a tight bandage on it. That horse is still eating his hay and oats."

Suppose something like that happened to old Moses – no, I just couldn't think of him being hurt.

"My boy Cubby isn't doing so good with hockey." This was the man who had forgotten his salt and pepper. I leaned forward. "He's kind of small, and the rest of his team are not much bigger. The other teams skate all over them."

Hah! Here was something to make a picture of. First, I need somebody to tell me how to play hockey. In last week's newspaper there was a Maple Leaf player, with short pants, long stockings and all.

"Here I come, Karl," I say, lacing up my good ol' skates.

"Now remember," he tells me. "Skate like the wind and low to the ice."

He taps me on the shoulder, and I'm off the woodbin into my picture. Right away I hack into a pass between two of the biggest kids of the other team that were so mean to Cubby's little team. They drop their sticks in surprise as this new kid, and a girl at that, whistles the puck in, the first goal for Cubby's team. Of course, that shakes up their goalie, too. He has been leaning against a goal post laughing at Cubby's team trying so hard to get the puck from all those big kids.

Karl is back there somewhere, watching the game but always ready if I need him.

The big kids are not used to somebody their own size against them, somebody with muscle from working like a man. They're scared and pulling every trick to stop me, but I know how to handle them all. I bang in two more goals, which evens up the score.

I get the puck again to put in the winning goal. I'm fighting the whole team, but at last I get set to score. Before I slam it in I see little Cubby with tears down his cheeks because he hasn't had even a play in the game. Karl sees it, too. He gives me a quick little tip of the head. That's all I need – I pass the puck to Cubby.

Cubby's tongue comes out and twists around as he tries to get the puck just right on his stick. The goalie flops around the ice desperately trying to stop him, but Cubby shoots the puck past him as good as I could myself.

Cubby makes the winning goal, so everybody goes wild over him. Me? Well, I get a little squeeze on the shoulder from Karl, so real I can feel it.

The door hinges, deep in white frost, screeched like they were hurting when the last wood-hauler came in from bedding down his horses. With him came a blast of pure coldness. It turned into a white cloud like the steam from a kettle and rolled across the room.

"Stepmother's breath," muttered one of the men, shivering as it swept over him. The cloud of cold washed over me, too, but I didn't so much as wiggle. Some things felt colder to me than anything of winter.

I shook myself out of my picture and slipped off the woodbox. I picked up some more firewood. It showed the three or four strokes it took me at the woodpile to chop each piece. A strong man would have done it with a single, clean cut.

Cubby's dad spread his blanket rolls on the floor. He tipped me a funny wave of his hand, something like an army salute, and I grinned back at him.

I threw the wood into the crackling flames and went through the door in the partition.

Mama sat on her big steamer trunk counting the money that the wood-haulers had paid. She asked me, in Old Country words, how many there were.

"Six, Mama," I answered in English. I turned to bolt the door and whispered to myself, "Six daddies."

CHAPTER 3

MAMA'S PET TALK

Mama had spread a yellow checkered cloth and a few dishes on one end of the big Old Country trunk. I sat on the other end to pull off my boots and put on a pair of wool sock feet.

The floor had lots of little mats sewn of brightly colored braided rags. I could hop from one to the other around the room and never have to step on the cold and splintery boards.

"It is so cold out," said Mama, stirring the saucepan of chicken stew on the heater. Beside the saucepan was Mama's coffee and a kettle of water.

Mama had hung the log walls with blankets of all kinds that she brought from the Old Country. The walls were warmer, but up between the rafters the lamplight made the frost sparkle in all colors.

"How many the eggs?" Mama asked.

"Four."

They were all there beside us, counting the one I found frozen and split open and now thawing out in a saucer.

I picked up two slices of bread and put them on the lid of the heater. A few crumbs fell and smoked. Their smell made me hungry for supper.

"The well," asked Mama. "Does it make the freeze?"

"I put the cover on, Mama." I turned the bread around to toast it evenly. "Besides, the water is way down in it now."

When the toast was a deep brown on both sides, I put one of them on a plate, and Mama spooned stew over it.

"How is the wood for the fire?" Mama put stew on her

own plate and broke off a piece of the toast to eat with it.

"Lots. All I ever want to chop." I lifted my plate to my lap.

When we had all the stew we wanted, Mama poured milk into my mug from a bright tin pail with a syrup label on its side. Sharp flat blades of ice rattled against the pail as she tipped it.

"For you," said Mama, filling up the mug with hot water, "the *kee-koo.*"

"Oh, Mama," I scolded. "I haven't said that for hot milk since I was a tiny little kid."

The scalding water melted away the frozen chunks and the icy 'I hate it' taste, too. Mama cuddled her mug of hot coffee in her fingers and asked me about the chickens.

"Their water pan freezes before they can drink much out of it," I said.

"I know," said Mama. "How is the big horse?"

"I have to bring more straw for Moses if it gets warm enough. And the stable door is freezing up, so I can't push it wide open."

"I know, I know," Mama said to that and to most of what I told her.

"Mama, how would you know? You haven't been out of the house since you went to see me at the school concert."

"It is the cold country," Mama said.

When my milk was done, I huddled over the heater and undressed for bed, holding up my sleepers in the heat above it. I hopped real fast out of my fleece-lined combinations into the baggy flannel sleepers with the moccasin feet that were so nice to my toes.

When I was pulling my clothes off, some of them felt a little bigger. Generally my clothes get tighter and tighter.

Was I grown up already?

Mama just laughed about it and poked her fingers into my back, "No, you still grow. It is the baby fat goes now."

Baby fat? Isn't that something! I started to hop away to my bed across the room. "Oh, my braids."

"Come, Karenne," said Mama. "I like to do it."

I came over between her knees while Mama pulled pins away and combed out the braids. I stamped my foot any time my hair got pulled.

"My poor little man." Mama brushed my hair until it was snapping, and little ends flew up as if blown by a wind. "So much work. Such hard work."

"Awh, looking after Moses and the chickens is no work. Chopping firewood isn't such a much either except for the big blocks I can't split with one whack."

"You miss your father," Mama said. "You never say anything, and you make the wake dream so much times."

I could have yelled at Mama for starting a picture about Karl when I didn't want one, especially about the way it really was with Karl banging out the door with his suitcase and me hurting on my bed but too mad to cry.

What Mama said was just her pet talk. Like I talk to Moses and Pokie. They don't answer me. I didn't answer Mama.

"Why do you have his long gray eyes?" Mama said, like it was mean of me to look like that. "Not my blue ones?"

I looked at Mama. Yes, her eyes were more blue and round than mine and Karl's. Her face was roundy, too, a pretty kind of round and not at all like Mertie's mom. That was round, too, but her mouth was always pulled up in the middle like she was mad and looking for somebody to be mad at.

Mama's hair was in a big soft bun with a roll around her forehead. Except for that she looked like a girl too big to have to go to school.

"Would you miss your Mama so much?" she asked me.

"How could I miss you, Mama?" I told her, starting toward my bed. "You're always here."

But, hey – this didn't sound like just pet talk. I went back and gave Mama an extra big hug and kiss for good night before hopping away to bed.

The fat straw tick crackled and rustled as I rolled up on it. Every time Mama saved almost enough chicken feathers for my bed, I got bigger and they weren't enough again. I lay there shivering, too chilly to sleep even inside my sleepers.

I made a nicer picture of Karl with his big warm arms around me. Right away me and the bed felt warm as toast.

CHAPTER 4

Moses, Pokie and the Woodpile

Mama scratched at the thick hoarfrost on the window until she got down to the ice on the glass, but she still couldn't see out. The sun was up behind the bush some place but not strong enough for us to get much light. She opened the door and looked out at the wall of poplar bush in white winter bark and black twigs along that side of the yard, then the other side where she could see the the well and the woodpile and some of the stable .

"It is so cold." She shut the door, just like she had really seen the weather.

She wound my long brown scarf around and around and over my toque so tight my nose was just a flat spot on my face. I held my arms out like I couldn't move them with my two jumbo sweaters, overalls, jacket and work coat all on me. How could I do any work with all this stuff on?

"You should wait," Mama worried. "Maybe it not so cold bye and bye."

"Mama, this is morning."

The wood-haulers were gone, and there were Moses and the chickens to feed. I looked into the woodbin. If I didn't bring in some firewood soon, the house would get just as cold as the outside.

Mama finished the knot with the fringes of the scarf sticking in my mouth, threw her hands up and turned away.

"Be careful of the big horse," she said as I went out the door.

My footsteps on the frosty snow crunched like biting into an apple. I pulled the scarf down on my chin and drew in a breath of the winter air. It was sharp with the cold and tangy with the smell of winter trees.

A loud whicker came from the stable.

"Shut up, Moses, you old monster," I called out. "You think you hear me coming to give you some breakfast, but I'm not."

I kicked the door hard a few times until it broke clear of the frost that sealed it around the edges. In the darkness inside I could barely see the white star on Moses' black forehead over the top rail of his stall. I hugged him around the nose, which was about as high as I could reach.

"Of course I won't. Moses is a bad old horse, so he doesn't deserve anything."

Moses snorted and shook my arms away. I walked in the darkness until I stepped on a pile of hay. Before I could find the hay fork leaning against the wall, Moses banged his hooves on his manger.

"No use to make a fuss. Nothing for Moses today."

I pushed the fork tines down into the hay and lifted, then down again until I had as much hay as I could carry. I held it above my head till I got to Moses' box stall and spilled it over the top into his manger.

"Oh, I made a mistake," I scolded as Moses snorted and began to crunch the hay. "That little bit is all you're going to get."

I brought two more fork loads, then grabbed him by the ear, scratching slow behind it the way he loves. I told him all the horrible things I was going to do to him when I came back with his oats.

Then I went out to the chicken house.

I opened the door barely enough to shove one leg in and push back the silly hens, who wanted to come out, winter or not. Then I had to push them again with my other leg before I could get inside and close the door.

I walked knee deep in Barred Rocks until I threw a tin of wheat and oats around the floor. The hens scrambled for the grains, their red heads hacking like little axes.

One hen stood a few seconds with her beak an inch above a kernel of grain, scratched mightily with her feet, then ate the grain.

I felt a few sharp jabs on my leg.

"Oh, good morning Pokie, you old darling," I said to a tattered old hen at my feet. "Are you going to dance and sing for me today?"

Pokie turned one way, then the other way, going *craw, kuk-kuk cra-aw.*

"That's just grand, Pokie." I picked her up for a special size of hug. "I'm glad to see you looking so well."

Pokie didn't look well, really. Her gray and white feathers didn't lay in neat rings around her body like the younger hens.

"Remember, Pokie, when I first made friends with you?" The bird, resting quietly in my arms, looked at me with first one eye, then the other. "Then you were just a fuzzy black chick with a yellow spot on your head."

Pokie gave me a love tap on my sleeve.

"You ran around for the longest time with feathers only on your wings. But after that you grew into such a beautiful hen and gave me an egg 'most every day. You always let me play with you."

I tried to stroke some of the crooked feathers into place.

"You got so old so soon – poor Pokie."

Pokie started to kick around in my arms. I put her down on the floor and gave her a few extra grains from my pocket.

When hens are too old to lay eggs, they become chicken stew. But I cried so much for Pokie that Mama let her stay as a pet.

The water pan had to have the ice banged out to fill it

with warm water, and I filled the feeder with dry mash. Pushing back the silly chickens again, I went out.

I walked around the pile of wood, poking at the blocks here and there.

"Now, woodpile," I said, "you better not expect any pet talk because you're not getting any."

All the little easy blocks were gone. Those that were left to chop were the big knotty ones. "How do you expect me to do anything with that stuff?" I said to the woodpile.

I stood a block on end and lifted the axe, its handle blackened by years in a man's hands, so high over my head I all but fell over backward. Down came the axe with all the strength and speed in my arms.

The axe bit into the wood but not far enough to split it. I shook the block off and swung at it again – even harder. The axe stuck again.

"You're just trying to get even by grabbing my axe," I said to the woodpile. I shook the axe, pulled at the block and bumped it around in the snow.

"Oh, I give up." I leaned on the axe to get my breath back. The block fell off by itself.

If I could only chop into the same cut again the block should fall apart.

Missed! And was the axe ever stuck this time! I threw it all into a snowdrift.

"I can't, I can't – I just can't." I could have cried. These chunks needed somebody big and strong and real good with an axe. Somebody like Cubby's daddy.

"What's the trouble, Corinne?" I hear myself asked.

"Oh, Karl, you know it's this awful firewood. You never told me how to do it the right way."

"I meant to finish the firewood before I left."

"You don't have to come back to chop wood for me, even in a picture."

"Come now. Do I look as mean as you think I am?"

"Hey, you're Cubby's daddy!" I look into his grinning brown eyes and polite face like when I took him some salt and pepper. "You make a great Karl."

He looks at the axe and at me.

"Now, now, you can do it," he says. "Hit it hard and straight and you will split it every time."

"That's what I'm trying to do."

"And trying too hard, I'd say. You're throwing yourself off balance. Try swinging that axe like you have a feather in your hands."

"A feather? That's silly."

"Not if you try it," he says and fades away.

The axe came down straight and fast in my hands. The block crunched and flew in two pieces. For a while the firewood hadn't a chance against my axe.

Then I found that I wasn't hitting the blocks hard enough to split them. Just enough to get the axe stuck. I was breathing hard, too, and my arms almost couldn't lift the axe.

"I should be there with you, Corinne," comes a thin, ghostly voice, "to do work like this."

"I hate it, I hate it." I threw the axe into the woodpile. I yanked my mitts off and slapped them on top of it, one then the other. "Why does another Karl have to come and mess up my pictures?"

CHAPTER 5

NOTHING FOR MOSES

Mama had bread and plates on the kitchen table when I came in from filling up the woodbin though it wasn't dinner time yet. Mama was looking after me like she would the menfolk in the Old Country, making it look like dinner was almost ready when they came in.

After we did eat, I waited a while, then started to get into my coat.

"You go out again today?" She put her hand on my arm. "Too cold – too cold."

"But Mama, I have to feed Moses and the chickens again and fix up the stable before more wood-haulers come."

"Yes, yes." Mama tossed up her hands. "Put on the warm clothes."

"Mama, it's winter, you know. The cold is nothing to be afraid of."

It was quite a while since Mama came from the Old Country, but she still didn't like the cold winters or the hot summers either.

"Is my little girl might freeze," Mama said. "Be careful of the big horse," with another pull at the knot of the scarf.

I was born in this country, so I can show any kind of weather that I'm boss. And I'm big enough to harness up Moses and do the chores.

When Moses first came he was spooky. He jumped from any little thing. He didn't like me such a much until I played with him and gave him stuff and lots of pet talk. When he got used to all that, Karl laughed and said I stole his horse for myself. I named him, too, after the man we got him from.

"Mama, Moses is really a grand old guy."

Mama turned away and rattled some dishes. I went out the door with all its hinges squealing.

I opened the gate to Moses' stall and went in. Moses hurried over to me with a soft whicker.

"No, I didn't bring you anything," I said with a squeezy hug around his neck. He slid his nose up and down my clothes, sniffing loudly, and shoved me around easy with his big muscles. He tickled, too, which made me giggle and twist around, but he still got closer and closer to what he was looking for. "Moses is a mean old horse, so he shouldn't have anything."

The daylight came through the frosted up window in his stall strong enough now that I could see him good. I rubbed my mitt over the four-pointed white star in the middle of his black forehead. He was the best friend ever: strong if I wanted help, nice to me if I wanted to talk with him and funny to play with.

"Stop biting my pocket," I scolded. "I told you I didn't bring you anything."

After he gave another sharp nip at my coat, I pulled out half a raw potato. Moses grabbed it in his teeth but was careful to push my fingers away with his lips before he bit it.

"Oh, boo-hoo-hoo, you big pig." I put an arm across my face as if I were crying. Moses turned to a corner crunching the potato.

"You stole my last bite of food. I'll starve to death right here in your stall."

Moses just swished his tail at me.

"Well, if you won't give me back my potato, I might as well get busy and scrape out the dirty straw." I bent to the work with a heavy six-tined stable fork.

Moses came back and nosed me up and down for another

tidbit. He pushed me back and forth, so strong and so gentle I couldn't help remembering Karl's big strong hands.

"You want to play rough, hey?" I dropped the fork and wrestled his head. Moses shook it in fun, pulling my feet off the floor. I hugged him real tight.

"Roughhouse, will you? How do you like this? I got you pinned good."

Moses lifted his head, his warm breath like the heat from a stove on my face. He pressed his big soft lip against my cheek and wiggled it a couple of times.

"Aw, gee, Moses, a kiss for me?" I picked up the fork. "For that I'll make you such a bed."

I piled all the dirty straw from his stall on a stoneboat by the door. Its poplar pole runners and plank floor couldn't be seen under all the straw piled on it. Then I carried in forkloads of clean straw from outside and spread it in Moses' stall.

"Now, Moses," I said, climbing up the rails of his stall to reach the harness hanging on a wooden peg, "We're going to pull that stoneboat out whether you like it or not."

Moses turned and dodged, and I followed him around the stall with his heavy leather collar.

"Don't be so smarty." I tried to shove the open end of the collar around his neck. "You think if you run away I can't get you harnessed."

I did lift the collar on his neck once, but when I tried to buckle it, standing on tiptoe, the collar plunked to the floor.

"Come over here." I led Moses over to the manger with my arm around his head. "All I need is something to stand on, then I'll fix you."

I laid the collar on the manger, then climbed up beside it. When I stood up, only the collar and me were there. Moses had walked away.

I yelled and chased him around without getting a bit nearer to putting the collar on his shoulders. Then sneakily, I laid the collar on the manger and went out. I came back with a hand behind my back. Moses came whickering to me.

"Oats, Moses. Do you want them?" I held my hand over the collar as he snuffed at it. "Then go get 'em."

I let the handful of oats dribble through the collar. His head went down after them. Quick as a flash I buckled the collar. Though he jerked his head around, the collar was on to stay.

Then I took the harness off its peg and climbed back in the manger. Moses had licked up the oats and was gone once more.

"Moses, you come back here."

'Back' was a word he knew perfectly. He stepped backward toward where I stood in the manger with the harness over my arm. Back and back he came until he bumped into the manger, creaking it under my feet.

"Moses, how can I put this harness on your collar," I yelled, "when it's away over there at your other end?"

I went around and around the stall with the harness, its trace chains jingling against my legs, trying to throw it on his back, which was a little higher than my head.

"Got you, you big monster." With a big leap on one foot to give myself the last inch of reach, I slid the now tangled harness across his back. "We've had our fun, but now we've got to work."

Moses waited with a deep sigh for me to buckle the harness in place. He pushed his head into the halter and let me lead him out of the stall and in front of the loaded stoneboat.

"There now." I hooked the trace chains to the stoneboat. "It'll do you good to get outside, out of this stable for a while."

Pulling his halter rope, I clucked my tongue.

Moses braced himself against his collar. His hooves slipped and pounded on the frozen stable floor. With a snap and crunch of breaking frost, the stoneboat began to move.

"Whoa," I yelled.

We had gone hardly a foot toward the door.

"We got to go slow and easy, Moses," I said. "The door is frozen and won't open all the way. Gitup – whoa."

The stoneboat hardly had time to move the second time. Moses didn't like me to stop him, just when he got the load started, and make him do it all over. He pranced from side to side, getting all worked up.

"A little easy so we don't smash the door," I said. "Gitup – whoa, whoa, WHOA!"

Moses started the stoneboat for the third time and shook his head so hard his forelock whipped around before he stomped out the door going faster as he went. I was supposed to be leading him, but it was like I wasn't even there. I had to jump away from his hooves and let him pull the halter rope from my hands. The heavy stoneboat banged the door with a splintery crash and shoved it wide open.

Across the yard and away along the snow trail went Moses with the stoneboat, breaking into an excited canter. I ran yelling after him, and it was sure no pet talk.

Before I could catch up to him, he stopped where we had to put the dirty straw anyway. His neck was held up high, and he was still snorting mad.

"Moses, what's the matter with you?" I grabbed the halter rope with a furious jerk. "Don't you know you almost stomped on me back there? And your hooves are big and hard as flatirons."

Moses snorted angrily.

"Well, maybe I did make it a little hard for you," I said as I put my arms up around his neck, "starting and stopping like that."

He shook my arms away.

"Moses, don't be so terrible mad with me." His nose went even higher. "There's nobody around to tell me the right way to do things."

We stood like that for the longest while, me snuffling from the cold or maybe because I was crying a little.

"Poor old Moses." I stroked his neck the way he usually liked. "Couldn't you be a little bit easy instead of trying to stomp all over me?"

He turned his head away.

"Well, then, stay mad at me and see if I care," I yelled. "You're as mean as Karl."

I was sorry I yelled at him, and it didn't do any good either. We stood there for the longest time in the cold, both our heads up high and mad.

Then Moses nipped at my coat with his teeth. I pretended I didn't even feel that. But when he shifted his feet as if he might pull the loaded stoneboat back into the stable, I jumped for the fork to unload it.

"Gee, Moses." I pushed the dirty straw off in a hurry and jumped on the stoneboat. "It's great that we're friends again."

He scampered to the stable all happy again, with me standing on the bouncy stoneboat like Karl used to ride when I drove.

When I got him unharnessed and back in his stall, I found a board and, trying to sing one of Mama's skippy tunes, nailed it on the door to fix the broken place. That didn't make it like it was before, but it was still a door.

CHAPTER 6

MERTIE GUESSES

Last night's bunch of wood-haulers drove away with their loads before I woke up. Cooking their breakfasts had about emptied the woodbin, so there I was whacking away at the old woodpile.

"Hi yah, there. Ol' Corinney's got to do a little work, hey?"

I didn't have to look around to see that the squawky voice was Mertie's. He came right up this time and didn't make a sneak of it.

"H'lo, Rabbit, did you snare any Merties today?" I was glad enough to rest my axe even to talk with Mertie.

"Hey." He didn't snap onto my come-on to have a fight. "How do you expect to chop any firewood with little love pats like that?"

"You think you could do better?"

"Let's have that axe," he said, grabbing it out of my hand. "Watch how a man would do it."

He stood a block on end, turning it a little this way and a little the other way, each time waving the axe up and down over it.

"Now look." Mertie lifted the axe as high and as far back as he could reach. "Watch this."

He swung the axe down, grunting to show how hard he was doing it. It just nipped the edge of the block, flew sidewise and bit into the snow.

"You're lucky you didn't chop your foot off," I told him.

"Your old axe can't be hung straight," Mertie grumbled, sighting along its handle like a gun. "I'll have to make up for that."

Starting the axe's swing somewhere behind his back and gaining speed as it came over his head, Mertie brought it down with all his strength.

It stuck, just like when I did it. I grinned into my mitt.

Mertie muttered a rough kind of word as he tried to kick the block off the axe.

"That's worse than calling it a rabbit," I said, ever so smarty, but even that didn't get him mad.

"Hey." he looked at me sort of sneaky. "Why doesn't your dad chop your wood?"

"You know he's not here."

"I mean before he went." He licked his lips, then, as if he had just thought of something, said "Why do you try to make out he never ran out on you and your mom."

"Because he didn't."

"Didn't he?" Mertie crowded up close, mouth hanging open as if he didn't want to miss a thing I might say. "Then why isn't he sticking around?"

"What do you care anyway?" I said. I was ready to swat him hard if he guessed again that Karl was taken to jail for bootlegging or to the crazy house for acting funny.

"Ma wants to know. I mean, she says he musta run away because he didn't tell nobody about nothing."

"He didn't have to, did he?"

How much of Mertie's sneaky questions could I stand? I picked up the axe and tried to bump the block off it.

"C'mon. You can tell me," he coaxed. "We're friends, ain't we?"

What kind of a friend did he think he was to stick my axe in a block and then poke mean questions at me?

"He went on a train," I snarled. "And he went by himself."

"On a train? That's rough."

"Why is that?" I asked. "Isn't that what trains are for? To ride on?"

"Yeah, but the cars are full of stuff so you can't get in 'em."

"Then how do you go on a train?"

"You ride on top like a load of hay."

"That can't be so."

"'Tis, too," said Mertie. "When I was in town once a train came along, and there was lots of guys riding on top of it."

"My Mama rode on lots of trains when she came from the Old Country, and she can't even climb on a load of hay."

"She wouldn't be much of a hobo, then."

"What's a hobo?"

"A guy that rides on trains, stupid."

"What do they want to ride on trains for?"

"Because they don't never want to come back."

I felt some tears trying to come again. Karl was gone. Would he be going and going, never to come back?

"Now then," said Mertie, his mean little three-cornered grin coming now he had me worried. "You was going to tell me about your dad. Wasn't he really took away for something?"

I was so blind mad I threw Mertie down and pounded him into the snow. He got away from me and hopped for home faster than I could chase him. He didn't so much as turn until he was through the back gate.

"My ma says," he yelled, "no guy would run out like that except he wasn't your real dad."

"I'll tell you now," I yelled back at him. "He wasn't taken away – me and Mama threw him out."

"Yeah!" I could see Mertie's mean three-cornered grin spreading his face apart. "That's just what Ma said in the first place."

CHAPTER 7

ADOPT A DAD

I went to the stable to have a talk to Moses right after I chased Mertie home. He usually comes right away, whickering how glad he is to see me and rubbing his nose against my coat. This time he was so busy chewing hay that he was no better to talk to than a bag of hay himself.

"You lost that little game, didn't you?"

Close behind me, and he doesn't even tap me on the shoulder to let me know he's coming, there stands Karl. Sure it is – that maroon bush shirt he wears without a coat unless it's awfully cold, the two big hands always ready to lift me up if some place is too high or to take something out of my hands if it's too heavy, and that strong, square face always with a grin ready to start.

This is the sharpest picture of him ever, and I don't want it. Not now.

"How could I have lost?" I say. "Mertie was awfully sneaky, but I told him nothing."

"You didn't? Well, what do you think he got from all his guesses?"

"Nothing. I mean a lame chin and a busted rabbit, but that isn't such a much for Mertie."

"That was before. How about now?"

"Well, me and Moses hauled out the dirty straw," I tell Karl. "He got terrible mad at me, but it's all right now."

"That was good work, but what about Mertie?"

"About the same as usual. He tried to show me how to chop wood, and we got into a fight."

"I don't mean that either," Karl says. "What if he believes what you told him?"

"Like I said before, I didn't tell him anything."

"But you told him you threw your dad out of your house. What if he thinks that's so?"

"Let him, if he's that dumb. The kids at school tell Mertie all kinds of stupid things just to watch him snap them up."

"You're not at school now. What you did could make a terrible mess."

"Why didn't you tell me what to do before I went ahead and did things all wrong?"

"Sometimes pictures are not enough." Karl turned quieter and drifted out of the stable like a ghost.

I rubbed a tiny tear onto my mitt and looked at Moses. Lucky old horse. He always has his hay and oats – and work, too – and never has to worry about what he might say sometimes.

In nicer times I rode on Moses' back, leaning way ahead to hold on by the harness hames, with Karl walking alongside, talking about the birds, the Old Country, the well and anything else I asked questions about. His big hands felt so great when he helped me on or off the horse's back or caught me when I came sliding down a stack of hay so fast I was going to smash deep into the ground.

"No guy would run out on you," Mertie had said. "Except he isn't your real dad."

I heard the girls at school talk about things like that. They said that their real dads must have been something better than muddy-boots homesteaders – maybe a prince or something. They said they were put where they live now when they were too little to remember.

"Moses, how do you get a daddy if you don't have one?"

Betty Fanson once told me about how the Fansons wanted a little girl of their own but didn't have one, so they adopted her. Betty is one of the nicest kids at school.

"Moses, how would you like to adopt a daddy?"

Moses turned for a long slow look at me, then went back to eating his hay. He wouldn't mind if I did.

"Who do you think I should adopt?" I asked.

Moses thought about it without missing a bite of hay.

"Of course," I said. "Mr. Henshaw would be the closest. Then I'd have Mertie for a brother, wouldn't I? He isn't such a much, but lots of the kids have nasty brothers."

Moses lifted his head and snorted hard.

That settled it, but what was I supposed to do now? Just walk up to Mr. Henshaw and say, "I'll be your girl. I'm big and I'm strong, and I can do lots of things if you show me how."

By the end of the day I still wasn't sure how I would tell Mertie's dad I was going to adopt him. Then Mama was a help without knowing it.

"Is no milk for the supper," she complained. "The little boy is not bring from the Henshaws."

Mertie hated to bring milk for us even more than he hated me.

"I – I'll get it," I said. "Right away."

"I get the pail and the moneys," said Mama. "Put on real warm, and do not make the fight with the nice little boy."

"Hah!" was all I said to that.

Mama unwound my scarf and put it on again her way. I scrunched through the snow swinging the tin pail and rattling the coins in it.

When I walked through the row of trees into the Henshaw's yard, Mertie ran from the house shaking himself into the sleeves of his mackinaw and smooching supper off his mouth.

"Whattaya want?" he snarled.

I held the pail up.

"You got your milk already," he said, loud enough to be heard inside the house.

"Didn't." I didn't want the fun of fighting with Mertie right now.

"Then you didn't pay for it, that's why."

"I got money here." I shook the pail real loud.

"Well, I'll see what Ma's about to do with you."

He turned toward the house, me following.

"Who asked you to come in?" He nearly chopped me in two with the door.

My nose wrinkled at a strong sour smell. The Henshaws never let me in their house when it smelled like that.

In a while the door opened a crack, and Mertie's arm shoved out.

"Gimme that." He grabbed the pail and shook it so the coins rattled. He slammed the door in my face, but I heard him say, "Yep, Ma, she brought some money."

The sour smell seemed to fill the air. Then the pail came out again, barely hanging on Mertie's finger. I took the pail of milk real quick. Mertie wouldn't care if it splattered in the snow.

"Now, beat it."

"Hey, maybe this milk's no good," I yelled as he shut the door quick.

"Huh?" The door opened again before it latched.

"Well, something sure smells sour."

Mertie started to come out for a fight, but somebody pulled him back by an arm, and the door slammed shut.

I walked away feeling like both crying and pounding Mertie to pieces.

I wasn't out of their yard, just into the row of trees, when I heard frosty hinges squeal some more. Mr. Henshaw's face stuck outside the door with the crooked pipe that was always in it. He looked sneakily all around but couldn't see me through the trees.

He came out and walked to his stable, his pipe giving out a puff of smoke every step. He carried a big brown-necked jug like the one Karl carried water in to drink when he was working in the fields.

If that was water in the jug it would freeze up so fast in his stable. But if it was bootleg stuff, he would want to hide it under some straw or something instead of sending Mertie out to keep people from the house.

Now was my chance to run up to him, while he was by himself, and tell him what I had come to say, that I was going to adopt him. I did turn back and take one step.

My foot slipped. "Oops, be careful Me, if you want any milk."

But how could you slip on just old snow? It looked white like snow, but it kicked hard and slippy like ice.

Then I saw something a little shiny over in the bushes. It was another syrup pail to take milk in, like the one I had in my hand except it was empty and had been kicked all to wrinkles. There was a little bit of frozen milk inside it.

Now, who would kick somebody's milk around in the snow out of spite? Always be careful what you say, Me, I told myself. Did you see somebody kick it? No? Then you're just guessing. Think about that.

I thought and thought about who it could be. But even when I got home, I still thought it was Mertie.

CHAPTER 8

BEANS AND PEANUTS

Moses waited in front of the house with the stoneboat, which I had cleaned off real good to go shopping. The sun poked through the tops of the trees, and there was no more wind than if the trees were blankets. Moses stood with one leg bent lazily and white steam from his breath hanging around his head.

"Mama, why did you give me this raggedy old blanket?" I dropped it off the grocery box that I carried to the stoneboat. "I can keep myself warmer if I walk behind than if I hunker under a blanket like a sissy."

"You walk, then." Mama stuffed the blanket inside. "Last time apples got freeze."

I sat on the box and picked up Moses' reins.

"You have the little grocery paper?" asked Mama.

"In this pocket."

"And the letter you must mail?"

"In my other pocket."

"And look at good when you buy the – "

"Mama, why don't you come to Avard's canteen and buy your things yourself?"

"No, the big horse."

"I can drive Moses."

"I fall off," Mama chuckled as she went back in the house. "No good we do not have the cutter to ride in."

"Gitup, Moses," I yelled with a shake of the reins.

Moses sighed but didn't seem to hear me.

"Get going there, you monster."

Moses' ears swiveled around like he wasn't hearing anything. I flicked him with the loose ends of the reins. It was hardly more than if I hit him with a couple of soft shoelaces, but it told him that I meant business.

He took a few stiff steps, trying to edge back to his stable.

"Come on, Moses. You want to meet some other nice horses in the Avard's stable, sure you do."

The stiffness in his legs began to loosen after we got out of the yard and on the snow trail. His head rose, and the *crunch-uncha, crunch-uncha* sound of his hooves was faster.

The trail took us past the Henshaw's yard. Mertie came rushing out, sliding into his mackinaw sleeves. He watched until me and Moses trotted past, then he went back into his house.

"That was mean, Moses," I said. "Mertie thought he heard a great big rabbit coming. Poor Mertie."

The stoneboat plowed into the snow, breaking off chunks and throwing them around my feet. Before we got to the first corner of the bush trail, tiny whirls of steam came off Moses' flanks and drifted back past my face.

The winter air and the poplar trees and even a horse doing his work smelled so cold and nice.

The trail broke out of the tangled bush and passed a cleared field. I could hardly see the trees on the other side through the winter haze.

I told Moses that was like a prairie where they say everything is bigger and better. Moses turned his head to listen to me.

A big pile of firewood poles almost covered with snow was there near the trail. "I bet that's the kind of house where a wood-hauler lives," I told Moses. "They come from the prairies to buy wood from us. They make houses out of it, like beavers. Watch and we might see one come out.

"It's great to talk silly to you, Moses, because you don't tell anybody else. You won't, will you, Moses?"

He snorted hard.

Moses jogged along, ears turning around to catch my words and the little sounds of the bush. After a mile or so there were more of those level cleared fields, some on the other side of the road, but you could still see that straight wall of poplars along the far side of them. Even when we would come to Avard's canteen, there would still be lots of bush.

At last we found it in the middle of a little clearing. The canteen was made of logs but was bigger than our house. Its one big window, which I could see into because it wasn't frosted up like ours, was full of axes, hats and last summer's flypaper.

Behind it was the stable, bigger'n ours, too, and the beginnings of the farm the Avards were clearing and planting in summers. I couldn't see all the other farms I knew were around there because the Avards hadn't cleared out much of the bush yet.

I stopped Moses in front.

"Oh, Moses," I hugged him around the neck. "I kept this as a surprise for you. When I go in I'm going to adopt Mr. Avard, like a new Karl, you know. And I'll see if he'll take you, too."

I went to unhitch Moses from the stoneboat and put him in the stable. In a minute I would be walking around inside to see and smell all the clothes and toys.

"Hey, there, you Kragh kid." Mr. Avard stuck his head out the door. "No room in my stable for your horse."

I looked around the yard. Except for my stoneboat there was only one sleigh and that was the one Mr. Avard used to bring stuff to sell in the canteen.

"Did a lot of people come on horseback?"

"Don't be smart. Tie your horse to that tree, and don't be too long with your business."

I didn't unhitch Moses after that, but wasn't it lucky I had that old blanket to put on his back.

Mrs. Avard followed me around the store like she thought I might steal something.

"I hope you understand," she said with a tight kind of smile. "You may carry out your business here, then you must leave immediately."

"Why?"

"Oh, we have heard stories about you and your mother. We can't have the likes of you or your family hanging around our place."

"What stories?"

"You must know what I mean. You can't keep such things from your closest neighbors."

"I don't know what you mean."

"Oh, little pitchers have big ears, and you can't tell me any different. The same with your neighbor's kid, and once a story goes in, everything spills out."

"Do you mean Mertie? Mertie Henshaw told you stories?"

But her jaw shut like a badger trap, and she wouldn't say a yes or no.

I laid Mama's list on the counter. Mrs. Avard got some things while Mr. Avard got others. Then Mr. Avard packed them all in two paper bags while Mrs. Avard made change.

They wouldn't let me even look at any of the things to wear hanging on the wall or the good things to eat in boxes on the counter or in sacks, with the tops rolled down a little so I could see what was in them. I could smell them all together but mostly an open box of salty peanuts. Karl used to bring me some every time he went to the canteen.

I went to the post office corner and put down Mama's letter and three cents. Mrs. Avard put a stamp on it though she looked like the stamp tasted bad because she was licking it for me. She gave me the mail tied up with a string, then both the

Avards seemed to crowd me along the aisle and out the door.

Outside was cold again, but I didn't feel half as chilled as when I was inside the canteen.

The blanket I put on Moses to keep him warm while he waited was trampled under his feet. I stuck the groceries in the box and put the blanket around them.

Moses pawed at the snow, in a hurry to get home to his warm stable. I untied him from the tree but sat on the grocery box to think.

"Shut up, Moses," I said, when he kept fussing around. "Can't you see I'm making a picture?"

Karl comes marching up to the canteen and bangs on the door till the logs shake.

"What's this," he roars like a giant, "about you Avards being mean to my Corinne?"

"Don't blame us, Mr. Kragh," says Mrs. Avard with a shaky smile. "You know we can do anything we want to your little girl when you're not around."

"What difference does that make?" Karl yells so hard the window rattles.

"Oh, my goodness, but you're big and strong," Mr. Avard says.

"Now that you are here, everything will be all right. You know how people like us and the Henshaws, and the wood-haulers always pick on anybody who doesn't have a good strong daddy to stand up for her. Especially when we were told that your own family threw you out."

"Now, who," Karl grabs each Avard by the neck, "told you a lie like that?"

"We're afraid to tell you because Mertie's dad might stand up for him. Besides, we didn't know it started as Corinne's joke."

Laughing like a giant, Karl shoves inside, picks up a handful of white beans and throws them in the box of peanuts.

"Oh, dear, that spoils our peanuts," say the Avards. "What can we do now?"

"Get Mertie," Karl laughs like a monster, "to pick the beans out of the peanuts, if he has enough brains to tell one from the other."

Mr. Avard had slammed the door so hard after me the latch didn't catch. I pushed it open a little. They were both in the back, where they always waited when there was no business.

I opened the door real quiet and scrooched behind a pile of boxes. My rubber boots made no noise as I went to the grocery counter, but Mr. Avard happened to see me.

"Hey, you Kragh kid, what are you doing back in here?"

I grabbed a big handful of white beans from a sack and let them pour into the box of peanuts. I stirred them with my hand.

"Get out of here. What are you up to?" He came running from the back.

I was so scared with him coming at me that I jumped and ran for the door.

"Oh, my peanuts!" He sounded like he was going to cry. "What am I going to do with them?"

"Get Mertie," I yelled over my shoulder. "He can pick the beans out."

CHAPTER 9

TRAIN TICKETS

As soon as we got home, I gave Mama the grocery box, then put Moses in the stable. When I came in the house Mama was reading the mail I brought, with tears streaming down her face.

"Mama, what's the trouble?"

"Not wrong," said Mama. "Is so happy."

"Why is that?" I know all about crying when I'm mad because I can't get what I want . . . and once when I got that terrible beating.

"The ticket for the train," Mama pointed to a little strip of cardboard on the table. "It is to come to the city for a week."

"Nice for you," I said.

Why should Mama be so happy about the city? Wasn't there something I should remember about the city? The harder I tried, the harder I forgot.

"For you, too, is the ticket." Mama slid a ticket with a green stripe toward me.

I pushed it back. "Why would I want to go to some old city?"

"You never see the city. You would like so much."

"I'm not going," I said with a stomp of my foot. "I have to look after Moses and the chickens."

"The Mr. Henshaw." Mama ran a finger along the lines of the letter. "We ask to look after while we go. He will take us to the train, too."

"I said I won't go. So I'm not going – never and never!"

"But your father – "

What I had forgotten boomed around me like thunder.

"Karl sent those tickets, didn't he? He wants to get me to the city, too, doesn't he?"

"Yes, it is – "

"And that's where he ran off to – the city." I said it like going to the city was worse than going to jail. "Of course I won't go to that place. Why did Karl go?"

"He goes to get job for the winter," Mama said. "Is to get the money to make better for us and for farm."

"How about all the money you get selling firewood?"

"So little money," Mama swung her hands out wide. "So much to buy."

"That's just what Karl said when he got so terrible mad and ran away."

Something came to me like one of my pictures but not a bit nice. There was me, and there was Karl. He grabbed me so hard his hands hurt me and threw me facedown across my bed and that hurt worse. But what hurt the worst – oh, I stop remembering the picture before that part comes.

Afterward he put his stuff back in the suitcase. I had yanked it open and thrown everything on the floor. Mama helped him pack it again. He went out the door without saying anything more or even listening to me.

Mama laid the letter in her lap and looked up to the rafters.

"Is that what you tell the people?" she spoke very softly. "He is run away?"

"I don't have to tell them," I snarled. "They tell me."

After a long quiet while for both of us, Mama lifted the letter again.

"His friend Judd does not use room one week." She went on with the letter as if nothing had been said. "Is the week we come to city, so you have Judd's room."

"I will not go!" I stomped around in a circle, shaking my arms and yelling, "Not, not, NOT." *Clomp, clomp, clomp* went my feet. Every once in a while I threw out a big loud "NO!"

Mama didn't say anything, just looked at me with her round blue eyes.

I forgot to put on my coat when I went outside, but I didn't feel the need of it. And the firewood blocks hadn't a chance against somebody who was mad in every muscle. I chopped them until I couldn't lift the axe any more.

I came in the house awful careful so the hinges didn't squeal. Mama wasn't in the kitchen part. I went to the woodbin, snow dropping from my clothes. I sat to think.

What about the city, anyway? Mertie knows all about the city because his Ma came from one. He said that people and their houses swarm thicker than mosquitoes in summer. Mertie told me that city kids are so tough one of them could lick our whole school, at least all the girls.

I made a picture of what it would be like if I went to the city. In the city they build houses high up, Mertie said, one on top of another. In my picture I try to see what one log house would look like teetering on the roof of another.

Most of the picture is of me and Mama going to the city, sitting on top of a train. Moses and Pokie will die before the week is over, of course, without me to feed them and give them pet talk.

When I come to the part where me and Mama see Karl – well, my picture breaks to pieces.

I opened the door in the partition a tiny crack. Mama had pulled out her accordion. She was sitting with it on her lap and the letter beside her on the big trunk.

I found my little stool and carried it over by the woodbin. I sat on it with my feet braced to hold it from wobbling.

The accordion played, ever so soft and sweet, an Old Country 'I love you' song. Then it changed to a ripping, kicking polka. The house seemed to dance to the music. So did the stove and even the woodbin.

I got up and danced too.

CHAPTER 10

WOOD-HAULER'S AXE

"Hey, Sammy, you're no good as a bush rabbit without an axe in your hands," one of the wood-haulers teased.

"We came with just one axe," his daddy, the tall man said. "He pesters me to come to the bush, but he'll be safer if he stays a prairie gopher."

Did these prairie people torment each other, too? I felt sorry for Sammy. When the men were going to the bush, I put my firewood axe into his hands without saying a word.

"Whoopee!" he yelled, running to his dad's sleigh. "Now I can be Paul Bunyan's axeman."

I had chopped enough wood for today. I just needed to finish filling the woodbin. Then I could sit around a while and wait to do the chores before the wood-haulers came back to the stable.

Not long after they were gone the door squealed open, and in came the wood-haulers carrying somebody with a bloody rag on his leg.

"Sammy here had a little trouble with his axe," said Cubby's dad to Mama, but with no grin now. "We have to patch him up a little so we can get him to a doctor."

Mama rolled her eyes, rolled her head and lost all the English she knew. I ran to the table and pushed off what things were on it. They put Sammy on the table and stretched out his bleeding leg.

"What do you need?" I asked.

"It wasn't my fault, Dad," said Sammy. "A little willow branch got in the way."

Sammy was more afraid of what his daddy would think than he was of his hurt.

"Any boiled water? Something to make bandages?" asked Cubby's dad.

I hurried around getting them and even some other things before he asked.

Mama went into the other room and sat on the trunk holding a towel to her mouth. She looked so scared and so sick that I popped a kiss on her face as I ran by with more white cloth for bandages.

The men spoke in slow and straight words, all their teasing and smarties gone. They talked the same way to me. Cubby's dad turned away to wipe sweat from his face. Behind him I saw a big wad of bandages dripping red right through them.

"We have to stop that bleeding, Charlie," Cubby's dad said to Sammy's dad. The worried looks on all their faces scared me. "It's all of fifteen miles to town. We can't take the kid like this."

"Karl, Karl," I almost called out loud. "Sammy is hurt and he might die, and it's all my fault for giving him that axe."

Karl's face comes out in a picture, and it's just as grim as those trying to help Sammy.

"Are you helping?"

"I'm helping all I can, but they need more."

"Then give them what you heard about."

"I know, but that was just for a horse," I say. "Anyway, they wouldn't listen to a kid like me."

"Then are you helping as much as you can?"

The picture of Karl flickers out like a match flame. "Karl, wait," I didn't want to be left alone just then. "What if it doesn't work?"

I couldn't get the picture back any more than I could get back into a dream. I went to the cupboard, took out a cup and filled it.

"What's this?" asked the man I handed it to. "What do you want me to do with this flour?"

"Flour? Hey, give it here. Great idea, Corinne," said Cubby's dad, then to the others, "Tom was telling the other day about using flour to stop bleeding. It worked on Tom's horse."

I waited on the woodbin. I began to feel a difference in the way they were talking and moving around.

"Not a drop of blood," said one, and he sounded almost happy.

"Yes," said Cubby's dad, rinsing his hands in a basin of water. His face looked like a new man. "All we have to do now is wrap Sammy up real warm and take him to the doctor for a few stitches."

Mr. Charlie hurried outside. In just a little while I heard sleigh bells and trace chains come tinkling to the door. They carried Sammy out, and I heard the bells and chains again. They sounded smaller and smaller as they went away, until there was nothing left.

The other wood-haulers came back and stood in a bunch around me.

"Now wasn't that something," said one, more about something he was thinking – all of them were thinking, I guess – than really talking to me.

"Will – will Sammy be all right?" I asked.

"Can't say," said Cubby's dad. "But we all did the best we could, didn't we?"

"I didn't mean to get him hurt," I said. "I forgot Sammy is a prairie goph – I mean, he isn't used to handling an axe."

"By the yiping piping, you were the sharpest little nurse we could wish for at a bad time."

"No, I mean – "

"Young lady," Cubby's dad put his hands on my shoulders.

"Is something still troubling you?"

"I gave Sammy a crooked axe."

"So that's where Sammy got an axe." He looked me up and down. "Well, I had it in my hands, and it's a good axe. Maybe a mite heavy for Sammy's size, and he wasn't a bit careful with it. Hmm, is that the one you have to use?"

The others looked at me and at each other. They nodded, a quick down-up like men do, then they all put on their coats and went outside. One of them, maybe it was Cubby's dad, squeezed my shoulder as they went.

"Mama – " I rushed into the other room. "Mama, they fixed up Sammy's leg and took him to a doctor."

"Yes, they go." Mama was coming to the kitchen. "I make all clean."

She wiped off the kitchen table. Now that the trouble was past, she was herself again.

"Mama! Mama!" I was nothing but a weak and wobbly call from the bedroom.

"Yes, Karenne, I hear."

"Mama, I feel sick – shaking sick."

I had to lie down a while, now it was all over, with my head on Mama's lap. That's why I didn't know until the next day that the wood-haulers went to my woodpile and chopped every block in it.

CHAPTER 11

To the Trail

I shivered outside the door in the cold and dark of real early morning. I had picked up only a sweater and my gum boots, but not for anything would I go back for even another sweater.

A yellow ball of lantern light bobbed in and out of sight over at the stable. The clink and tinkle of harness chains made loud echoes in the bush, where there should have been no sounds at all.

The first team came past, heads proud and going at almost a trot. They looked, against the night snow, like the horses we cut out of black paper at school, with legs swinging on pins. Behind them came their wood-hauler, his arms higher than his shoulders to hold up the reins and one leg and another coming out ahead of him. He looked like a walking 'K' there in the dark.

If I looked just a little harder into the darkness, I could see the sleighs loaded with long firewood poles, a different black against the shadowy black of the bush behind them. The horses and man lost themselves in the blackness, except for the jingling harness, crunching snow and calls of "Back up" and "Whoa."

More shadowy teams and men came crunching in the snow to the waiting sleighs. I shivered from excitement as much as from the cold.

"Load's too heavy and the trip's too far," I once heard a wood-hauler say as the men from the prairies talked about their tumbled loads, broken harnesses and blizzards on the way home. "But you got to have firewood."

The sky was changing from dead black to navy blue. I could see the horses better now, pawing the snow and snorting clouds of breath like steam. The drivers went around hammering each sleigh runner to break it loose from the hard frozen snow.

"Well, boys." A man stood up on his load, his breath whirling about his head. "Are we set to pull out?"

"Weather looks good," said another. "Hope it holds."

The first team pulled hard on its sleigh, scrambling and stumbling as the frosty runners still held to the snow. They leaped back, then bounced ahead against their collars. The runners broke free with a groan, and the first sleigh was on the way out the gate, runners ripping the snow. One of the horses broke into an excited canter.

The next team started with the driver's clucking sounds and shouts. They followed the leader's sleigh tracks exactly, the tips of their poles clawing the snow behind the sleigh when they climbed up a little out of our yard to the snow trail.

In turn they all slipped at a half-trot around the first bend in the road. The sounds of sleigh bells and crunching runners came back thinner and thinner until there was nothing left to see or to hear. I went in the house.

I fixed up the fire from the red coals the wood-haulers left. Then I sat on the woodbin and spread out so I could soak up heat real fast.

Mama came into the kitchen with her hair tumbling down over her shoulders.

"You get up so soon," said Mama. "No school it is."

"I watched the wood-haulers go," I told her.

"It is the cold ride for the men," she said.

"Why, I think it would be great to go – " I clapped my hand over my mouth.

Mama looked puzzled, the way she did when I said some

English she didn't understand. Then she smiled.

"Yes," she said. "The city you will like."

In the stable later I make a picture of me and Mama riding on a train. I'm not sure what a train looks like or how big it is. The picture comes out a lot like we are riding horseback on old Moses.

"Here is the city," says Mama.

Karl jumps down from a house piled on top of another and grabs me by the arm.

"I'm going to give you a beating," he says in a hard voice, "every day you're in the city."

I try another picture where I'm riding – not with Mama, but on a wood-hauler's sleigh.

"Here is the prairie," the wood-hauler says, stopping his sleigh beside a big pile of firewood and snow.

Karl comes out a door in the side of it and grabs up a firewood pole in his big hands.

"Now," he says, "I'm really going to beat you."

Real quick I picture another Karl to help me. I find myself running back and forth, not sure which Karl is after me and which is supposed to help me.

"Moses, neither of my pictures was such a much," I told him. "Now I don't know what's best for me to do."

CHAPTER 12

Cubby's Dad

The wood-haulers come about twice a week if the weather and the sleighing are good. I thought Cubby's dad wasn't coming any more, but at last he was there, cooking his supper on our stove.

"See, Corinne, I didn't forget them this time." With that brown-eyed grin, he held up the salt and pepper from his grub box.

I looked and looked at him all the time until I went in to my supper with Mama. He was big, if not as big as Karl, and always nice. Cubby was lucky to have him for a daddy.

I waited in the kitchen as long as I could, then was so slow at getting my sleepers on that Mama was in bed first. I wasn't sleepy either, and I stayed awake until the lights were out in both parts. Then I got out of bed again, rolled my clothes in a bundle and sneaked out to put them behind the woodbin.

Real early next morning, when the wood-haulers were out in the stable, I pulled out my clothes and put them on. I put on lots of outside clothes, too.

I walked real quiet to the outside door, but before I opened it, I tiptoed back again. Mama's breathing was still slow and even. I hung my pendant on the bolt of the door with a kiss on one of the 'K's,' Mama's 'K.'

"To help you understand," I whispered.

I couldn't see anything from under the blanket roll on a wood-hauler's sleigh – did I really climb, in the dark, on the sleigh belonging to Cubby's dad? What if it was another wood-hauler's?

The first team of horses came snorting and rattling their

trace chains. Would I get caught hiding on the load of wood before it even started?

There were yells, bumps and thumps and crunching snow everywhere around. I had felt sort of scared when I just watched the sleighs go. I felt so terrified now that I almost screamed and jumped off, especially when I felt the sleigh start with a jerk.

At first I felt like we were going to tip over, or I would at least get rolled off into the snow. The horses' hooves pounded and slipped, and my driver yelled till I thought we might not make it to anywhere. That was just in our yard. Then we climbed to the snow trail with the poles under me turning and twisting like they might catch me by my arm or leg.

At last the runners smoothed out under me like they were on the main trail, but that scared me worse than ever. I never rode on anything like a big wood-hauling sleigh, just our little stoneboat. I couldn't even see if we were going out to the big prairies.

I poked up a corner of the blankets, just enough for one eye to look out. The bush was sliding by – nice old bush. At least that much wasn't scary. I took lots more looks while the light got a little brighter, but there was still more bush along the road. Did I miss the prairies, or were they really so far away?

I don't know when, but I looked straight up into the eyes of Cubby's dad.

"How did you know I was here?" I asked him.

"You snore like a pig."

I sat up. The sky was like clear blue ice. There wasn't a tree to be seen all the way to the sun, which looked like a smashed egg over at the edge of everything. And snow, snow, snow – miles of it!

"Is this the prairie?"

He nodded.

"Cold isn't it?" I pulled up the blankets against the wind. It could push a chill through all my knitted and woven clothes as if they were netting. Now I knew why the wood-haulers came in sheepskin or buffalo coats.

"My turn to ask questions." I hadn't seen him look so severe any time before. "First, what are you doing here?"

"I hear a lot about the prairies." I waved my hand at the miles of plain snow. "I never saw any."

"I see. Now, why me?"

I thought he'd be glad to have me come. I'm big and I'm strong.

"Because of Cubby," I said.

"Cubby, eh? I suppose that should make some sense," he said, like it didn't to him. "Does your Mama know where you are?"

"She's going to the city for a nice time. She doesn't want me."

"Strange that she would." He looked at me real hard. "Why wouldn't you go with her?"

"She's going to Karl. He ran away last fall and only wants to beat me."

"Sure must have changed. I talked to him last fall, and he was full of what he was going to do for his farm and family."

"If you don't believe me, ask anybody. Ask Mama."

For a long while, or so it seemed, he just stood there, looking down at me.

"Say, how are your feet?" he asked suddenly.

"All right, I think." I wiggled by toes inside the gum boots. "Not very cold."

"Get off," said Cubby's dad, stopping the horses.

I started to cry.

"No, no. I wouldn't pitch a dog out in weather like this." Again that brown-eyed grin that made me trust him from the first. "We can't have any frozen toes, can we? So hop off and run behind until you get yourself warmed up."

His strong young horses were faster than poor old Moses. I had to hoppity-skip sometimes to keep the sleigh from running away from me. When I felt warm all over, and a little out of breath, I scrambled up on the moving load without asking him to stop.

Cubby's dad looked like he was worried about something. He looked straight ahead on the empty trail.

"I'm fine now," I said, which made him jump.

"Good," he said, handing me the reins. "Mind keeping an eye on the trail for me while I jump off and warm up, too?"

I took the reins from him, proud that already he thought I was a useful girl.

As the sun came higher, it looked even more like the yolk of an egg with the white gone all smeary. Two sun dogs, like pieces of rainbow on each side of the sun, seemed to make the cold feel colder.

The horses followed the turns of the road by themselves. So well that, while I was looking around at all the prairie, I forgot what I was supposed to look out for.

Some wood-haulers' sleigh had upset and scooped out a bad hole in the hard snow of the trail. I saw it just as the horses were about to step into it.

"Whoa, whoa, WHOA!" I yelled, pulling as hard as I could on the reins.

The horses didn't stop. They were used to only the voice of Cubby's dad. Their forefeet were already stumbling into the the bad part of the road. If the sleigh followed them, it would surely roll over.

"Haw, then," I yelled again, pulling the rein with all my strength. The team swung to the left, glad of the better footing I steered them into. The sleigh leaned over as it went around the bad road but not enough to uptip.

"That was great, boys," I told the horses. "Now let's get

back onto the trail."

A pull on the other rein and they were back on the good road again. Cubby's dad jumped back on the sleigh.

"Couldn't have done it better myself," he said. "You're going to be awfully hard to turn down."

He took the reins so I could hunker down out of the cold wind. He sat on his grub box.

"Do you mean I can do things real good?"

"You're as sharp a youngster as I've ever seen," he said, shifting like the box wasn't comfortable. "But – "

"Tell me," I said, "about your little boy, Cubby."

"He's a little hellion, of course," and he laughed.

"Lots of boys are, well, full of life. I'm used to that."

"You are? Well, he certainly makes things miserable for his sisters."

"Sisters? You have some girls, too?"

"Three in all. They spoil him rotten."

I said nothing more. Three girls! What would happen now to my picture of a being a great sister to little Cubby?

CHAPTER 13

COLD PRAIRIES

The horses' hooves went *tidilla, tidilla,* like a sewing machine stitching miles and miles of road behind us. The snow road was packed hard as ice from so many wood-haulers hauling their loads on it.

I looked back, and the bush was only a low blue streak along the edge of this place of nowhere.

"How much farther is it?" I asked. I was getting tired of so much prairie.

"We're barely started," said Cubby's dad, looking around at me like Karl used to when I did something all wrong. Not mad at me for it, mind you, but like I made an awful mess anyway.

The more prairie I saw, the more cold I felt. I jumped off the sleigh and trotted behind to warm up some more.

So Cubby had three sisters. Wasn't that something! I tried to make a picture of what I would do with three girls, but I didn't know any of them. Besides, I was too cold to make pictures.

Then comes a picture without me trying to make it, a picture of the girl in the well, and she's crying. Why? She's back there in the well, and I'll never come to holler down to her.

"Hey, Me, just look at this." I pointed to a farm beside the trail, which had a great big stable, three or four chicken houses or maybe some granaries, and a big tall house. "Wouldn't it be something to live in a place like that?"

Not one of the buildings was made of any logs. Mertie was right, they did make houses on top of one another. What he didn't know was the bottom one had no roof when the other one was put on top.

I ran up and grabbed one of the load stakes, got a foot on the end of the bolster and swung myself on the load of poles like I had done it all my life.

"Is your farm like that one?" I asked Cubby's dad.

"Much the same," he said, turning to look. "House painted a different color."

"Great. I'm sure I'll like it."

"Why do you say that?" He looked at me.

"I mean, if you have two houses on top of each other, there's lots of room for me, and a big stable like that is going to have a lot of horses and chickens and things I can look after."

"Is that why you hid in my bedroll: to look after my livestock?"

"Not altogether. I need to talk with you about the rest."

"Go ahead, talk with me," said Cubby's dad.

"Really I – I mean." This was harder to say than I thought. "I want to adopt you."

He didn't say anything for a long while.

"I asked you before," he said. "Does your Mama know what you are doing?"

"She doesn't care if I don't go back," I said quickly.

"I asked you if she knows. Why are you so sure she doesn't care?"

"She didn't try to stop Karl from going away."

Cubby's dad sat on his grub box and just let his horses take me farther and farther into the cold prairie.

"Adopt a dad," he said, mostly to himself. "And I thought that with four kids I'd heard everything possible."

"I don't think I talked about it the best way," I said through chattering teeth. "You don't seem to like the idea."

"I think I understand just fine." He looked at me real careful. "Now, looks like the winter is still getting to you.

How about another dogtrot to get your blood on the move?"

I wanted to talk to him some more, but he stood up like he wouldn't listen.

"You don't have to stop the horses for me," I told him. I still had my pride.

"As you like," he said. "Watch you don't get run into by that wood-hauler coming this way."

The wind was getting stronger and chasing snakey streams of snow over the fields and across the road. Instead of getting much warmer, I felt colder than I ever had in the bush. Then the sleigh stopped so suddenly I almost ran into the ends of the firewood.

The other wood-hauler drove his empty sleigh right off the trail to give Cubby's dad room and stopped too. They talked away while I waited. I couldn't even tell what they were talking about, likely pigs and crops and things while I stood there shivering.

What a big silly Cubby's dad must think I am – trying to adopt him when Cubby already has three sisters. It made my teeth chatter even harder.

"Corinne!" called Cubby's dad. "Corinne, come up here, will you."

I scrambled through the snow. Here on the prairies the snow was not deep, but it was crusted over and lots harder to walk through. I would have liked to hook my arm with Cubby's dad, but he hadn't really answered about if I could adopt him.

"Care for a ride on my sleigh, Corinne?" asked the other wood-hauler. He was tall as anything standing there with the collar of his big coat strapped across his mouth and his nose hid by white frost.

I shook my head. Who was this other man anyhow?

"Charlie's a good fellow," said Cubby's dad, feeling my cheek to see if it was freezing. "He'll look after you better than I have."

"Oh, Mr. Charlie!" So he was, though bundled up so it was hard to know him. "How – how is Sammy?"

"Healing well and feeling topnotch, all thanks to you," he said. "Now how about a lift back to your home?"

"I can't do that." I was blubbering from plain cold.

"Can't you?" said Cubby's dad. "How do you see that?"

"I said I was going to adopt you."

"I see, and a promise is a promise?" He rubbed his chin. "But does it have to be in such miserable weather?"

"Would it be better if I wait?"

"I don't see why not," said Mr. Charlie, making a warm nest of hay and blankets on his sleigh.

I stood shivering, waiting to hear what Cubby's dad would say.

"Of course," he said, "I could say hello to Cubby for you, and you could come out to see him this summer."

I was so cold I couldn't even feel their hands lift me onto Mr. Charlie's sleigh and tuck me deep into his hay and blankets.

Cubby's dad's horses were getting cold, too, and jumped at taking his loaded sleigh away.

For a while Mr. Charlie kept asking me if I was warmer, was my nose freezing or my feet? Then the hiss and little bumps of the sleigh runners did it to me again. I went to sleep.

"Here we are," said Mr. Charlie. "Oh, Corinne – hey, Corinne!"

That got me wiggling in the blankets. I didn't have any dream to put away, so I just opened my eyes. I saw bush, bush and bush all around and even almost above me. We were right at our front gate.

"How do you feel?" Mr. Charlie asked, sort of anxious.

"Warm as toast." I climbed off the sleigh and looked

toward the house. I sure didn't feel like going in, especially by myself. What would I tell Mama? What could I say about what I had done? Little bush rabbits might get caught in Mertie's snares, but even they are not stupid enough to run out to the prairies.

"My apologies for not driving you to your doorstep," said Mr. Charlie. "This time I pick up a load of wood elsewhere."

"Oh, that's alright," I said. "I can walk in, I guess."

Still, I waited.

"Anything more I can do?" asked Mr. Charlie.

I wished that he would come in with me. A daddy, even Sammy's daddy, would be so much better to explain things to Mama.

"Thank you, but I guess not." I walked slowly into our yard and called back, "Thanks for the ride."

What should I do? Just walk in and ask Mama if dinner is ready? No, better I should see if Moses and the chickens were fixed up before the wood-haulers came. I didn't suppose Mama would really go out the door in the cold and do the chores. Maybe I could show her I'm needed to do things around the place.

But what if I had made her good and mad at me?

I walked around the corner of the house without knowing what I should say.

"Chickens!" I said. "Chickens all over our yard."

CHAPTER 14

MOSES OR POKIE, POKIE OR MOSES

The door of the chicken house was open, and the snow was full of Barred Rocks pecking at nothing in particular.

"You stupid things," I scolded them. "Are your feet so cold now you don't feel it any more? You get right back into your house. Come, Chippy-chip-chip."

I coaxed most of them inside the chicken house by calling them and spreading a little grain on the floor. All of them went in but two stubborn pullets who stood deep in the snow as if it was summer grass. I jumped at them, flopping myself in the snow, and caught them one in each hand. I pushed them, flapping and squawking like crazy, into the chicken house with the others.

I heard a sound like a snore when I was busy with the chickens. It came again from the stable.

"Moses, what are you doing?" I called, a little worried. Moses didn't even whicker back to me.

I ran to the stable.

"Oh, Moses, Moses!"

He partly lay on the floor and partly held himself up with one front leg, the one that was all black. He had a rope around his neck, and it was pulled so tight by his own weight it was strangling him.

"Moses, how did you ever – " I tore at the knots in the rope, one at his neck and one where the rope was tied to a rail of his stall. They were hard and with so much of his weight on them, I couldn't loosen them.

"You should never have run away, Me," I told myself.

Moses gave another strangled gasp, and his eyes rolled wildly.

"Moses, I've got to go get the axe – "

I ran toward the woodpile and nearly tripped over a silly old hen that I had missed putting back in the chicken house.

It was Pokie. She had hopped into the deep snow and stood with her feathers fluffed up and neck pulled in from the cold.

"Moses can spare another second for a sick old biddy. Upsy, Pokie, and I'll take you where it's warm."

I stooped to pick Pokie up in my arms like I had done a thousand times. She jumped from my hands and flew away.

"You shouldn't run away from your best friend," I screamed at her. "Moses needs me worse."

Pokie flapped her way over a big snowdrift, nearly falling into it, and settled into the snow beyond.

From the stable came the sound of hooves thumping the floor and a strangled try to scream like a scared horse does. I had given Pokie all the time she could have.

I ran the rest of the way to the woodpile and back. In the dark of the stable after the sun outside, I could hardly see anything. I chopped so hard the axe stuck in the rail. Moses thumped to the floor.

He lay there, not moving. Was I too late? No, his ribs lifted a little and he made another choking sound. The other end of the rope was still tight around his throat. With his weight off the rope, it should be all loose.

Hey, this knot wasn't the kind Karl had showed me to tie a horse with, the kind that can't tighten on his neck.

I threw my mitts off. For a second my hands felt as big and strong as Karl's.

I poked and pulled at the knot, but my fingers just couldn't loosen it. I tried to move the rope a little so it wouldn't be quite as tight on Moses' neck. He only made another choking sound.

Moses didn't need to be tied when he had a box stall. And Mama, even if she had come out to the stable, wouldn't tie Moses up, especially in such a crazy way. It was a slip knot, the knot Mertie made in his rabbit snares.

I leaned back and pulled at the rope. It moved along his neck a little bit but not enough to help. I grabbed the knot in both hands. I was so blind mad I didn't know what I was doing or going to do.

Mertie should be in a snare himself. He should. He should for just once. And if I had him in my hands right then I would . . . the knot came loose.

Moses gasped loudly.

He lay on his side, his ribs heaving like he had run miles. I threw the rope away like it was a snake that might bite again. He wasn't all right, at least not yet. His eyes were rolled back so only the whites showed, and he wasn't moving his legs, except they were trembling. Then he sort of coughed, which was a whole lot better than that scary wheeze.

"I'll be back in a minute, Moses," I told him. I couldn't do any more for him right now.

Pokie hadn't moved from where she landed except to spread her wings and tuck her head in her feathers like she was sitting on a nest.

"C'mon, Pokie," I said, scooping her up from the snow. "This is no place for a sick girl like you."

Pokie's head fell down and hung across my arm.

I screamed. Her eyes looked so clear and open it was hard to realize that Pokie was not still there behind them. I knew lots of chickens, and some had died. Pokie was the only one I ever made friends with, and I just never thought a friend would die.

When I came back, Moses was still lying down but with his legs folded under him. He looked more comfortable, but when he tried to stand up for me he dropped back down, just too tired.

"Here, Moses," I squatted down and held out my hand. I could have cried right then. "I brought you some chicken mash. It won't be so scratchy for your poor throat as oats."

He licked the mash from my hand. I teased his forelock and talked to him with my nicest pet talk.

When he had all the mash, I stood up.

"I'll get you some warm water to drink, too," I promised. "You have to get all right, Moses. You're my only best friend now."

I picked up the piece of rope again and looked at it. If anybody but me or Karl went into his stall, they'd get kicked or stepped on good. Lots of times Mertie said he could tame any horse, mostly Moses, but I wouldn't let him try it.

I poked around in the manger and found some sticks and string that I sure hadn't put there. And a handful of oats that had been licked at but not finished.

"I don't need any brains to figure it all out," I told Moses. "Somebody put a rope in your manger, like I do with your collar, and poured these oats under it. Then you, you big simple, stuck your neck in it."

What about the chickens running around in the snow? Why did I think at first Mama tried to look after the chickens and left the door open? Poor Mama.

I tossed the rope on the stoneboat of dirty straw.

The chickens would be Mertie's spite after he couldn't do anything with Moses. I was ready to bet on it. But as I went out in the yard I remembered again how Karl said I might be wrong sometimes. Prove something before I pop off my temper.

I walked around the stable and chicken house.

"Hey!" I bent over a scratch in some smooth snow by the chicken house. It was a figure '8' as neat as if cut with a knife blade.

I poked my hand deep into the snow. I felt something and pulled it up. A wire. A rabbit snare. That was all the proof I needed.

When I came into the house, Mama didn't seem to hear the hinges squeal. She was sitting on the bed with something in her fingers. I sat on the trunk and saw it was my pendant that Mama was holding.

"Mama, about Moses and the chickens – "

She didn't move, though she seemed to know I was there.

Never mind, Me, I told myself, if I tried to tell Mama about it all, I'd bawl so much I couldn't say anything anyway.

We just sat for the longest while, looking up into the rafters.

"Mama," I said in a real small voice.

She turned her head with eyes all red like mine.

"Mama, could I – could I still go to the city with you?"

She put out her arms. I slipped between her knees like to get my hair done. I got hugged instead.

"My man, my big little man," Mama said.

That was just some pet talk, and I didn't have to understand it.

CHAPTER 15

Mertie's Snare

This picture is no good for me. I have two people in it, and they are arguing with each other.

Not Moses, who is feeling pretty good now considering what had happened to him yesterday. He chewed his hay and paid no attention to me or anything else but that hay.

"Before you pop off at Mertie like you want to," Karl says, "remember he'd like nothing better than to get you steaming mad. If you do something foolish, then so much the better for Mertie."

"No," says Me, who is flat on the wall like she usually is on the water. "Mertie almost killed Moses, and that isn't just having fun. Corinne has to give him some of his own medicine, or he'll only get worse."

"Then she'll be no better than he is," Karl says. "And what if Corinne goes too far?"

"With a monster like Mertie," Me says, "it would be only what's coming to him."

"Hold your horses, both of you." I hold up my hands, then point at Me. "If I snare Mertie, and good, would that show him something about doing nasty things?"

I get a nod for what I say and turn to Karl.

"Now, what if I do something to him that doesn't hurt him, unless he hurts himself and then it's his fault?"

Moses snorted real loud, which sort of blew them both away. Well, Moses liked the idea, and who was it got hurt in the first place?

I picked a hammer off a nail by the door and went plowing through the deepest snow ever along our back fence. I found what I wanted at the corner, a piece of tough old barbed wire about as long as I am tall.

Back in the stable I took down the rabbit snare I had hung on the same nail as the hammer.

"If I don't get mad that'll spite Mertie to death," I said and took a good look at the snare. "Hmm, I can make one to look like that."

With bangs and 'ouches' as the steel stickers stabbed me lots of times I hammered the barbed wire into a big '6' like the little rabbit snare. Then I hung both of them on the nail and waited at the door.

I heard the echoes of his feet come crunching in the snow. Yes, here came Mertie short-cutting past our stable with two rabbits he'd caught today.

"Oh, Mertie," I stepped out of the stable and called him. "I want to ask you how to do something."

"Yeah?" He came a little closer, though he stood out of my reach. "To do what?"

I went in the stable to bring out the little snare. Coming back I bumped Mertie who was sticking his nose in the door to look at Moses gobbling hay.

"Hey, what – ?" he said, grabbing at his pocket where he had some other snares.

"Found this around somewhere," I grinned, though inside I was boiling to jump at him and pound him to little pieces. "I want to know, how do you make these things work?"

"Like this," he snared his mitten over and over like a big smarty until I should know for sure that he was good at snaring rabbits. "And put it some place where rabbits go."

"Great, if that's all there is to it, then mine are fixed right."

"You set some rabbit snares?" he said. "You got to make 'em out of wire. How did you do it?"

"Like this," I said, bringing out my barbed wire monster.

"Haw, haw," said Mertie, shoving both his rabbits through

the loop. "You can't catch a rabbit with a thing like that."

"Who wants an old rabbit?" That's when my mad started to come through. I grabbed the little snare out of his hand and snared my mitt over and over. I must have taken out some of my mad on that mitt the way Mertie hopped back from me. "There's a bigger sneak than that coming around our place. That's who I'm after."

Mertie put up his arms around his neck and backed away from the piece of wire.

"B – but," he said, "you can't do that."

"Suppose I don't know I can't?" I was real smarty. It was the first time I got Mertie afraid of me, and I liked that.

Mertie looked around the yard.

"Where did you set your snares?"

"How can I remember so many?" I sort of waved to the big willows at the back gate he'd have to go through to get to his home. I looked at him as mean as barbed wire myself.

Mertie looked at my snare, shivered a little, then hopped away.

He stopped by the willows. I watched his head turning as he looked them over very carefully. Then, beating the air ahead of him with his arms, he worked his way along the path between the trees. Once in the clear beyond them, he went home at a run.

"Moses," I said, while I was finishing up chores in the stable, "I just fixed it so nobody sneaks around here any more." I opened the door to go back to the house when I saw Mertie's mom, her coat thrown across her shoulders, walking real mad to our house. I went back in and did some more work with the dirty straw.

"Corinne," Mama called. "Corinne."

In the house Mertie's mom was sitting on just the edge of a chair and talking so fast that nobody, especially Mama, could make out what she was saying. I sat on the woodbin, kicking my heels against it and twisting my fingers.

"Corinne, tell true me – " Mama said.

"Nasty little brat . . . horrible thing to do . . . my poor Merton," Mrs. Henshaw gabbled.

" – you make trap from the wire?"

Mama was confused, most likely by Mrs. Henshaw's fast gibbering more than what she was saying.

"Hundreds of them, my Merton tells me," Mrs. Henshaw cackled on. "Stuck around every place. He's scared half to death – just plain murder."

" – to hurt your friend Mertie?" Mama finished.

I wished it was the girl in the well sitting here on the woodbin. Mama mustn't be told any fibs. But it wouldn't be fair to let Mertie sneak out of the snare he had really set for himself.

"Wh – at!" I shrieked. "Did Mertie tell a whopper like that?"

I giggled and giggled and giggled. Mama turned from me back to Mrs. Henshaw.

"Did you see these thing yourself?"

"Of course, I didn't." Her mouth snapped shut like one time when her top teeth fell down on the bottom ones. "Do you think if I found one . . . then got caught in it . . . I'm alive and well so far as you can see."

Mama's mouth closed, except for a little wiggle at the corners.

"I wonder where Mertie thinks there are those kind of snares?" I said to Mama.

"Right in those big willows at the back," Mrs. Henshaw told Mama. "Merton said he had to shove them aside to walk through there."

I still had my coat on. I hopped around and around the yard like Mertie. I crossed the yard to the willows and danced in circles around them, in them, and if I could have

I would have danced on top of them.

"There!" I said when I came back.

Mama was alone. I stopped giggling when she turned her round blue eyes on me.

"Where did she go, Mama?" I asked her.

"Is to home," Mama said.

I hadn't seen her anywhere between our place and hers. I went out of our house to look again.

Mertie's mom stood in the open door of the stable, her head tilted to look up at the nail where the snares had hung when I snared Mertie. She didn't see a thing because I had buried the barbed wire snare under the dirty straw.

Mertie's mom stamped out of the stable mad as a hornet fly. I squeezed myself against our house where she might not see me. She went to the willows where Mertie thought a snare might be hidden. I thought she was looking for a lot of snares. Instead she broke off a mean-looking switch and cut the air with it a few times.

I shook a little but not from the cold. A switch, all the kids said, hurts worse than a spanking.

But she turned away and, with the switch up on her shoulder like a sword, marched off to her home.

I went to the well and took off the cover.

"Remember, Me, I told you I won't hurt Mertie," I said into it. "Just take a look out here who's going to do it for me."

CHAPTER 16

CRY IN THE WELL

The well was crying. I could hear it. Long desperate howls with a screech once in a while, real scary because of the well's big, whoomy sounds.

Moses was strong enough today to pull out a load of dirty straw. When we went to the well for his drink, he stopped, pointed his ears at it and pranced around as if he might jump and run.

"Easy, Moses. Steady boy."

The cover was off the well. It wasn't like the wood-haulers to do such a thing, to let the well freeze up. Then I saw a dead rabbit lying in the snow.

I held onto Moses with his halter rope and looked in the well. Mertie stood knee deep in the water, twice as far down as I could ever reach him. His mackinaw was soaked with the cold water, and he was scared.

"Corinney," he blubbered when he saw my face. "Get me out of here. I'm freezing to death."

"Serves you just right," I blasted at him. "I should just drop rocks on you for what you did to Moses."

"I didn't mean to." With his chattering teeth and the echoes in the well I could barely hear what he said, but he sure knew what I was talking about. "I was just trying to tame your horse for you, then he got the rope caught in the manger and wouldn't hold still for me to fix it."

"Moses doesn't need any taming. How about when you let the chickens out in the snow. Were you trying to get your lasso on them, too? Poor old Pokie died then."

"I didn't touch your old hen," he said real quick. "I

couldn't find you nowhere around, even in the chicken house. And I already got such a hiding because you laughed at Ma. Don't leave me down here."

"Maybe, just maybe I'll try to get you out," I said, like I was only thinking about it. "I'll go get your dad."

"No, no," and he began to cry. "Get me out right away."

"It's not far." Why was I starting to talk nice to Mertie? "He'll be here in no time."

"No, he's too busy to come," and he cried harder. "Besides, he'll give me a harder hiding. You got to pull me out, Corinney."

I walked two steps away from the well. He yelled like murder until I came back.

"Don't go away like that," he screamed. "Stay here with me."

"I just went to get the well rope." I dangled it down to him. "Hold on tight and maybe I can pull you out."

"Don't go away any more," he scolded pitifully. "When I can't see somebody, it's awful down here."

His hands were so cold and stiff he couldn't hold the rope. I tied the pail onto it and let it down again.

"Step into the pail, then up you come."

With Mertie in the pail, and water, too, I pulled and yanked my hardest. If I braced my feet against the side of the well I could lift him some. When I reached to get another hold on the rope it slipped back.

We both cried – Mertie from the cold and me because it was no use. Besides, the rope hurt my hands even through the mitts.

Moses whickered in my ear.

"Oh, Moses, you monster," I laughed, a mixed kind of laugh with tears running down my face. "You want a drink now?"

He pawed the snow. I looked at him and stopped all my

crying.

Of course, I never think of the best way before I waste a lot of time with the wrong things. Now I felt as rock-steady likethe time Moses was strangling to death, or when Sammy was bleeding so bad.

"Hold on, Mertie," I called down the well. "Help is coming."

I unhitched Moses from the stoneboat and backed him to the well.

"Oh, I didn't ask you, Moses," I said. "Are you still mad over, you know, what happened to you?"

"What did you say?" Mertie yelled. He could hear me lots better down there than I could hear him up here.

"Nothing," I said. "Just telling Moses to pull you out of the well."

"Tell your horse I didn't mean anything. I been wishing I didn't fool around with him in the first place."

I tied the well rope to Moses' harness and led him forward. The pull of the rope turned his collar against his sore neck, and he wouldn't try. Next I tied it to his trace chains, but they caught against his legs so he couldn't walk.

"Mertie, you know what?"

I was going to tell him that I couldn't pull him up. Then he really would scream, and I could sit back and let him suffer. Like he had to with that big switch his ma took home, only in a different way.

Moses turned partly around so he could poke his big face into mine.

"Moses, what are you trying to do?" I wiped away the frost he rubbed on me. Darned old horse, when there's trouble he always trusts people to know what to do.

"All right, Moses," I patted him on the neck. "You just gave me an idea. Turn the rest of the way around here."

I put his head almost over the well and tied the rope to

his halter.

"I've seen you lift a wagon with your halter," I told him. "Mertie is lots smaller, and I'll help."

Then I yelled down the well, "Hang tight, Mertie."

He babbled something I couldn't make out, but he was waiting in the pail, steadying himself with the rope. He must have been getting cold from his wet clothes.

"Back up Moses – back," I said, pulling on the rope, too.

The rope slid up out of the well with me and Moses pulling on it.

"Back, Moses, back up."

Mertie came up good at first, then he stuck near the top of the well. Only his head and an arm came out. I grabbed his mackinaw, but I just couldn't pull him any farther.

"Keep going, Moses," I yelled. "Back up – back!"

Moses pulled hard, forefeet braced and eyes rolling from the strain of the halter on his head.

"We just about made it. Back just a little more, Moses."

Mertie started to slide down into the well again, pulling me with him.

"Moses!" I screamed. "Keep pulling."

He had his head down, chin almost in the snow. When I yelled at him Moses reared up on his hind legs, his fore legs pawing the air.

The rope slid up again fast as lightning until, just when the pail with Mertie's feet in it was coming out of the well, the rope broke. But Moses' mighty yank tossed Mertie and the water in the pail in a big splatter over me.

"Oh, Moses," I said, hugging his neck. "You did it, just you yourself."

Mertie could only roll around in the snow until I helped him stand up. Even then he walked like his feet were round on the bottom.

"C'mon, Mertie. Mama will soon get you all dry and

warm."

"Ba – ba bub," was the best that Mertie could talk, he was so cold. I understood he meant no, he wanted to go home.

I pushed him on the stoneboat and hitched Moses to it again. I spanked Moses faster and faster, snow spraying high from the jumping stoneboat. Mertie rolled around like a sack of potatoes until I sat on him to keep him from rolling off.

Mertie's mom ran out the door as soon as Moses' hooves hammered into the yard.

"You little demon," her voice was squeally, and her hand was lifted up like she was going to hit me. "What have you done to my Merton now?"

"Fished him out of our well," I said.

"I can see . . . soaked to the skin . . . such a cold he'll have . . ." Mrs. Henshaw gabbled. "Why did you put him in there, you nasty thing?"

Mertie's dad came out with a brown-necked jug in his hand like he had been doing something with it and forgot to put it down.

"I'll get to the bottom of this," he said, waving the jug around. Some brown stuff slopped out on his hand. "Merton, what did she do to you?"

Mertie was so cold now he couldn't even shiver.

"Is this the way you treat your friends?" Mrs. Henshaw started to talk. When she starts she can talk and talk.

I rolled Mertie off at her feet. He just lay there and couldn't move.

"Gitup, Moses," I said.

Then they both picked him up together. Moses trotted the stoneboat back to the well.

"That's right, Moses. You didn't get your drink yet. You broke the rope, you clumsy, so the pail is down at the bottom of the well."

Moses whickered and banged his hoof on the trough.

"Yes, yes, all you think about is your water. I'll see what I can do."

I looked into the well for the longest while, trying to figure out what had happened. The pail hadn't fallen to the bottom of the well. It was there at the top, snared in a tangle of cords, string and a few sticks.

That smarty Rabbit sure sets his snares 'most anywhere. He made this one to catch my pail so I couldn't lift it out of the well. Mertie fell into our well while he was fixing his snare in it. It would work, too, just like when me and Moses tried to pull Mertie out of the well.

Moses banged the trough with his hoof.

I took the pail out of all the stuff and tied the broken well rope together. I pulled out the sticks and strings and tossed them on the stoneboat, then let the pail down the well.

"Here's your drink, Moses." I poured the first pail of water, muddied up by Mertie falling into it, in the trough. "Hope you don't mind the taste of Rabbit."

When Moses drank all the water he could hold, I looked down the well.

"What do you think, Me?" The muddy water in there made the reflection brighter than anything. "What should we do with Mertie?"

She still had a few wrinkles running around from when I was dipping water out.

"He could have killed himself just trying to make me feel stupid. Should I tell his ma, or maybe Mr. Henshaw, too?"

The wrinkles in the water stopped, and she looked into my face so clear and steady.

"I know, I know, you'll say enough's enough," I said and jumped on the stoneboat. "Gitup, Moses."

When Moses pulled the stoneboat back in the stable, and I pulled his harness off, I shook my finger under his nose.

"Now see here," I said. "You're not to tell anybody what happened at the well or about these sticks and string I'm hiding under the dirty straw on the stoneboat. Don't tell even Mama."

I finished what I had to do and went into the house. I had just got my work coat and overalls off when the door hinges squealed again. Mertie's dad came in.

He went to the woodbin and turned his pipe upside down to blow some mud out of it. Then he sat on a chair and took out a pocket of tobacco and stuffed his pipe ready for his walk home. He had that sour smell hanging around him he had lots of times.

He talked to Mama about crops and weather and stuff. I wanted to walk away to our part of the house. Mama pulled me back.

When his thumb couldn't poke in another crumb of tobacco, Mertie's dad stood up.

"I come down here," he said, "to shake this little feller's hand."

That's just what he did, with me standing sidewise and as far away from my hand as my arm would allow.

He put the pipe in his mouth, cracked a red-headed wooden match with his thumb nail so it lit with a bang, then lit his pipe and went *fuff-fuffing* out the door.

Mama didn't ask what Mertie's dad meant by what he did, nor did she say anything at all. But every way I turned, Mama's round blue eyes were looking at me.

I said nothing either, nothing at all, until I was in my sleepers, and Mama was brushing my hair. I just had to tell Mama something – nothing to scare her, of course – about Mertie and the well.

"Mama, suppose you did something big for somebody, like save that somebody from drowning? Though that isn't it, mind you."

Mama waited, hair brush up for the next stroke, asking no questions. Just those eyes looking at me.

"I mean, would that make it so you can't fight with him anymore?"

CHAPTER 17

Little Red Accordion

Me and Moses stopped by the house to listen to Mama playing a happy polka on her accordion. He turned his ears to the sound and stuck them there. I never knew that Moses liked music. When I sing to him, he snorts and whinnies and makes awful noises.

Why would she take out her accordion now? Except for the one time she got the train tickets, she hardly looked at it since way last fall.

Before that she used to play it most every night to me and Karl, whether we danced to the music or not. There she would sit, rocking a little from side to side in time with the music, with a great big smile on her face.

"So happy," she'd say, while she was trying the fingering for the next tune. "So happy, me."

Moses had a wise look, but he couldn't tell me why she played her little red accordion.

Everything was just the same, except Karl wasn't here. He was sometimes, even for Mama, a big piece of trouble. Then, why wasn't she happy all the time now? The accordion was right there for her to pick up and play.

"I remember now, Moses," I told him when I took him to the stable. "She's going to the city to see Karl. That's tomorrow, isn't it?"

Moses nodded his head and wriggled his upper lip.

"Are you sticking up for Mama? Or are you trying to shake your bridle off?"

I slipped the harness off him, and Moses found his way into his stall.

"Let me tell you something, Moses." He crunched his hay real loud like he wasn't listening much. "I might have promised to go to the city, but I never said I won't be as scratchy as an old porcupine."

I came into the house quiet and went to the woodbin. Mama was in the other room, her fingers dancing on the accordion buttons. The tickley little between-notes made my foot tap on the floor, in spite of myself.

Since that letter came, Mama's mouth was smiling most of the time and her eyes all the time. Today her accordion was laughing for her.

I couldn't make a picture of what a ride on a train would be like. I hoped Mertie was right that I'd ride on top of it. Then I'd freeze to death in a couple of miles and wouldn't have to go to the city.

Yesterday two suitcases came out of nowhere and waited on the floor by the trunk. Now my two dresses, my white cable-knit sweater, lacy nightie and some more of my good things in the closet were gone. So were a lot of Mama's clothes.

I was thinking so hard about all this that when Mertie's dad knocked on the door I jumped like he was chopping it with an axe.

"I come down here to see about your chores," he said. "Where's your ma?"

The music finished, and there was the sound of Mama putting the accordion away.

"Going on a trip, little feller?" Mr. Henshaw sat down and took his pipe out of his mouth. "Where are you going?"

"Nowhere," I said, remembering how hard Mertie tried to find out where Karl went and why, "but I might like the ride."

"Like the ride, hey? Haw, haw, haw."

Mama came in with her handbag and sat down at the table with Mr. Henshaw. I heard a lot of money being counted. Soon he went home without saying anything more about chores.

I waited on the woodbin awhile. Then I banged through the door into our part, picked out a few heavy woolies and looked around real slow.

"Where's a suitcase for me?" I snarled.

Mama pointed to the small one.

"This dinky thing?" I popped the lid open. "It's full of stuff already. Is this where you put your accordion just now?"

Of course, I knew the accordion was back in its box under the bed.

"I take not accordion. Is much to carry without accordion, too."

"Anyway," I said, poking around in the clothes, "there's not a thing here I want to wear."

"Some I packed in mine," said Mama. "These to make you look the nice little girl."

"But a freezing one," I said, waving the winter stuff I had on my arm. "These are not packed."

"Oh, me." Mama rolled her eyes, and then she rolled her head. "I must find the box."

"I'll do that." I grabbed a cardboard box that said 'Pork and Beans' on it. I turned it upside down. Spoons and pie tins and stuff went clitter-clatter on the floor. "This will have to do."

Mama put her hands to her head and ran out to the kitchen.

"That's great, Me," I said. "Now we can pack everything our way."

I tied up the box my way, too, winding it round and round in heavy binder twine with big knots every turn.

"Oh, my child!" Mama said when she saw it. "How can you make loose the knots?"

"I can get what's in there," I said, still snarly. "Nobody else better try."

That night, when Mama was trying to straighten a tangle in my hair, the comb got stuck. I got mad and ran off to bed with it in my hair. Then the straw tick crickled and crackled so awful loud I couldn't sleep all night.

I was busy driving a team around and around a field in summer.

My horses were Moses and Karl, who was in the other harness because I needed two horses for the work. Karl was all sweaty and tired from working like a horse.

A girl climbed out of the well with a pail of cold water hanging on her arm. She held it for Karl to drink, then poured the rest of it over his head and arms like I used to.

"Who is so mean to do this to you?" the girl asked Karl.

"Corinne is not mean," Karl said, "except she won't listen to anything I say."

"Hi there, Me," I yelled. "You live in the well, but you can't come out like that."

Neither of them heard a word I said. I picked up something from the ground.

"Here is your accordion, Mama. I'm sorry that Moses stepped on it."

"It does not matter any more," said Mama. "I play not accordion when I can't be happy."

I never slept a little bit all night.

CHAPTER 18

To Nowhere – with Mertie

"It is the chinook today," said Mama at breakfast. "We ride warm to the train."

Even inside we could feel a warm wind blowing outside. The frost among the rafters was melted into some wet spots. Outside, the snow was so soft it didn't crunch. I made a snowball, which I tried to make Moses think was a potato.

When I came in from the morning chores, Mama was sitting on the trunk with the alarm clock on her lap.

"Did you see the Mr. Henshaw?" she asked.

"No, I didn't. Why?"

"It was time to go to the train and we sleep."

"Mama," I looked at the clock. "It's only ten minutes past ten. We have lots of time."

"It is so," she said after a look at the clock herself. "Why do I think it is ten minutes before two?"

All the going-away clothes were on the bed. Mama put hers on, coat and all, then took them off.

"The green dress is better to see when come to the city." She changed it, then put her sweater on me in spite of my squawks.

"You must make the ready, too." She tried to put my sweater on herself.

"Mama, what is the matter with you?" I scolded. "You're doing such crazy things."

Mama stopped running back and forth and looked hard into my face.

"You are excited," she said, "because it is your father you go to see."

"I don't want to see him, remember? Besides, he wouldn't want me either."

Mama threw her hands up and let them drop the way she does when there's something she just can't explain.

"Come." She picked up the hairbrush. "We make the pretty Old Country girl for city."

She braided my hair, and I couldn't stop her.

"Sleigh bells," I said. The sound came faint but clear from over in the Henshaw's yard. I tossed on my going-away coat and ran to the stable.

Mr. Henshaw came jingle-jangling into our yard with his team of smart black horses and a greeny-black cutter with blood red runners.

"Corinne, come," Mama came outside and called, scared they would go without me. "Corinne!"

I came from the stable with a tear drop hanging from my eyelashes.

"We must not make late the train," Mama scolded, picking some of Moses' hairs off my coat. Most of them dropped on her own coat.

"My horses will get you there in plenty of time," said Mr. Henshaw, real proud, and tucked the suitcases against the curved dashboard. I wanted to hold my pork and beans box, but he yanked it from my hands and put it with the other stuff.

"Guess you can pile in," he said, rolling back a heavy buffalo robe with green baize lining.

"Hi, ol' Corinney." Up popped Mertie's head with a grin exactly like one I cut in a pumpkin last Halloween. "Wanta ride with me?"

"No, I sure don't."

"Why, Merton, how did you get in there?" His dad sounded all puzzled.

I thought, but didn't say it, somebody better kick him out

of the cutter before he messes up the trip.

"Is the little boy to come?" Mama asked. She had paid money for the cutter to get us to the train.

"Might's well," Mertie's dad mumbled, "seeing as how he's come this far."

Only from his house to our house. Did he think Mertie might lose his way home? And I had to sit in the middle, right beside the little monster.

Mertie sat awful quiet for him. The horses' hooves spanked away miles of snow, and still he did nothing, and did nothing and nothing.

"Mertie, are you dead?" I asked him.

I was all set for him to yank my hair and other things he was good at, but this was meaner than any of them.

"Top foot," he said, all of a sudden. I felt his foot on mine.

"Oh no, you don't," I said, pulling my foot away.

The boys play that game at school, mostly when everybody is just standing around. If they can step on somebody's foot and hold it, then they can say, "I'm the boss."

The buffalo robe humped this way and that way as me and Mertie tried to get at or get away from each other's feet. His dad kept on driving, but Mama rocked around like a boat in the sea she always told me about.

"Tish," she said to me. "You shake the blanket and make cold my legs."

Mertie got too stompy. I tried to slide my feet so far away he couldn't find them. Then I lifted them right up on the seat and sat on them. Mertie thought I was just quick at getting away from him so he tried to get quicker.

"Got you," he said, with a big thump under the robe.

"Ouch, my corn!" Mertie's dad roared. "What in thunder are you kids up to?"

"She started it," Mertie whined.

That was a barefaced fib, but I didn't say anything. I was

scared to because this wasn't our cutter, and we needed it to get to the train. Mama didn't say anything either, but wouldn't it have been great to have a daddy on my side of the cutter just to say, "No, Mertie started it."

"I know plumb well who started that fool game." Mertie's dad picked up his foot to squeeze a big dent out of his boot. "And I know plumb well who smashed my toe."

He looked at Mertie, who was trying hard not to laugh, "Let me tell you, some of these days . . ."

If he was mad at Mertie that made two of us. He never said much of anything when Mrs. Henshaw was around, especially to Mertie. Now he was started, he went on and on until the runners of the cutter bumped and scraped over a road running crosswise to us with two iron strips along it.

"Yon comes your train," said Mertie's dad. He pointed with his pipe to a black dot with a little smoky pile over it that the railroad track sort of pointed at. He drove us over to the train station, and me and Mama got out of the cutter.

That was a train coming? Well, I thought, if you're going to ride on that dinky thing, Me, you can only sit on top of it, and even then your feet will drag in the snow.

But the train grew big as a house and ran by hissing and yowling like a tremendous cat. A big school bell clanged away on top of it. Behind it trailed a cloud of stinking smoke and a row of big red boxes on noisy wheels.

"Awh," I said. "The train missed us."

"We do not ride on the engine," said Mama. "Here comes the train."

Everything stopped with screeches and groans. At the end was a green car full of windows.

"Come," said Mama, picking up the suitcases. We had to walk along a platform to some iron steps on the end of the green car. "This one we go."

A man wearing a flat-roofed hat with a tin thing on the

front of it that spelled "CONDUCTOR" came down the steps, put a stool on the platform and stood beside it to help Mama bump her suitcases all the way up an iron railing beside the steps. He grabbed my bean box and handed it over the railing to Mama, then half ran into the station. I stepped on the train myself.

"Goodbye." Mertie's dad waved his pipe.

"And good riddance," said Mertie.

I had nothing handy to murder him with, so I just turned and stuck out my tongue at him.

"You know what you look like?" he said. "You look just like your old horse with his tongue hanging out."

"Mertie," I yelled, jumping off the train. "I'll rub your smarty face in a snowbank."

The engine snorted and pawed to get started. A rattledy-bang came running along the boxcars back to our car.

"Corinne!" Mama called.

"Gonna stay behind with me?" Mertie had that mean three-cornered grin.

"I should," I said, trying to yank him out of the cutter. "I don't trust you to look after Moses if I'm away."

"Oh, I'll look after him good," said Mertie, hanging onto the cutter.

"I'll see to that," said his dad.

The conductor came back, grabbed the railing in his hand and yelled "Bo – ard!"

"How do I know that you'll be nice to Moses?" I asked Mertie, though I felt a little better after what he said. "Look what you do to me."

His bottom lip straightened out, and he really had a nice smile. "Moses is a nice guy."

"Bo – ard!" came again from closer.

"And I'm not? I've got a mind to – "

The conductor grabbed me by the collar and carried me

to Mama just like my bean box.

He yelled "Bo – ard" one more time, and the train started. I went to follow Mama through the door.

Bang-kersplat! A snowball on the side of my head plastered my braids so full of snow there wasn't any left over to fall down my neck.

"Mertie, you sneaky rabbit," I yelled, going to jump off the train again.

"Tish," said Mama, shoving a suitcase against my legs so I couldn't. "It is only the boy fun."

I was still mad, but I carried my pork and beans box inside and along between two rows of two-people chairs made of hard straw.

Mama stopped by two empty ones. She put the suitcases on one and sat on the other. I put my bean box with the suit cases.

Me and Mama dug all the snow out of my hair that we could. Then to get even for Mertie's snowball, all I could do was make a picture. How about stuffing him into his mom's big butter churn?

Good enough! I jam on the lid with the dasher in it.

Hey, this picture is great – I even hear a *Ka-plap, ka-plap* as I thump the dasher up and down on Mertie in the churn. The wheels under the train go *Ka-tick, ka-tick.* That isn't really the sound I am hearing, but it does help to make a good picture.

CHAPTER 19

WHAT CAN YOU DO WITH A TRAIN?

I squeezed over to the train window.

"Ow!" Mama yelled when I stepped on her toes. "Is better ride by the window?"

"Awh, the window's so full of ice I can't see out anyhow," I said, scraping it with my fingernails and breathing on the little hole I made. "All I can see are things like shadows flying by."

"Here, little girl." A man leaned over the back of our chair and scraped the window with a big farmer's knife. "You can see now."

Everything looked just like when I was riding on the sleigh with Cubby's dad, only it was going by faster.

"Prairie, and lots of it," I said, and looked around for something else to do.

I found a tin place at the end of the train where I could get all I wanted to drink by pushing a button printed 'Water.' Then I had to run to a little room at the other end to take care of all the water I drank.

Something was keeping the car warm, but what?

There wasn't a kitchen stove or a wood heater anywhere. Hid in a little room at the end was a big round iron thing with firelight flickering through its holes. It didn't have any woodbin, but right beside it was a pail full of black stones.

"Look, Mama," I said, holding out what I found. "There's a big stove back there in the corner but no firewood to put in it. What are these black things?"

"Which black things?" Mama was tired and grumpy. "The

coal or the hands? Uh uh, do not wipe on the clean dress."

I ran to the little room again and washed the black off my hands with the cutest cake of soap and some water that kept trying to jump out of the washbowl.

"Mama, what can I do now?"

"When does the child ever get tired?" Mama moaned. The nice man who scraped the window for me heard her, and he chuckled.

"Poor Mama," I put a kiss on her cheek. "I'll sit with you for a while."

The next thing I knew, people were crowding past our chair, bumping me with their suitcases. Mama was trying to wiggle into her coat with my head on her lap.

"I wasn't sleeping, Mama," I said as I jumped up and grabbed my pork and beans box.

"Sure, sure." Mama was rested and smiling now. "Now you ready for the city?"

We came out of the train into the night, but not in the dark because of the big lamps everywhere. I walked with Mama through a lit of people until all of a sudden I found I was alone with my bean box. No people, no Mama.

I went back a little and found Mama kissing a big man. He wasn't wearing bush pants and a mackinaw. He had a necktie and a long coat like the dudes in the mail order catalogues. But he was Karl all right.

"Oh, here's Corinne." When he saw me he put out his arms. I turned sideways with my face pushed against my shoulder.

"H'lo," I said, my nose up in the air and my eyes looking down at the dirt on the ground. He didn't touch me.

Another man with a flat cap like the conductor, except it spelled 'TAXI,' put me in a car beside him like I was the Queen of Sheba. Mama and Karl had to go in the back. I never saw a car except in pictures, but I rode in it just like I knew how. The car took us a long way from the train. Two bright lamps on the front showed me a lot of things we almost ran into.

We stopped in front of a house like the prairie house I saw once. I mean it wasn't made of logs and it was lots of houses one on top of another. Inside, we walked up steps and steps until I was sure the house was twice as high inside as outside.

"Here we are," said Karl, stepping through a door to light a bright little lamp dangling from the ceiling.

The room was shaped like a letter 'L,' going one way to bed and drawers under the slant of the roof and the other way to some kitchen things and a little window, now dark except for spots of light outside. The table and a couple of chairs were scratched a lot, and they were so old and dirty they were black.

"Mama?" I put my hand on a bench padded with leather. "I suppose this dinky thing is my bunk."

"Corinne will have Judd's room," said Karl. "It's across the hall by the bathroom."

We went to look at the room, which smelled of tobacco and men's clothes. I peeked into the bathroom, too.

Mama and Karl went back to his room talking Old Country. I ran into the bathroom.

It's lamps were great. So was everything you might use for fixing up, like after a smoky train ride. I leaned over the washbowl, and I could see into the looking glass ever so clear and bright, lots better even than Me in that dark and ripply well. I wiped a coal smudge near my ear and fixed up a braid that was sagging like a clothesline. I felt I could look around at the back of my head if I wanted to.

"It's great to see you here in the city," I said. "You're no giant-killer to chop wood easy as a sneeze, but you're no fatty little baby either. You're just – oh, you're just Me and that's great."

Mama and Karl stopped talking in the room. I ran across the hall, but I was too late. The suitcases were open and Mama was unpacking them. Karl stood with his farmer's knife in his hand and my bush sweater in the other. The pork and beans box was open with cut cords all around.

"No, I did not bring," Mama said. The light reflected all red on Karl's face from the opened box. "Is only Corinne's cold clothes, not accordion – oh, Corinne, CORINNE!"

Karl looked from the accordion in the box to Mama, then to me. He gave me a tiny nod, a quick down-up like the wood-haulers did after me and them fixed up Sammy's leg.

And Karl winked. Sure he did.

CHAPTER 20

BABY FAT

Mama squeezed her accordion closed with an awful squawk. Her music hadn't been much better – no happy, tickling notes and jumping dance tunes.

"I cannot play the nice tonight," she said. "I do not know. I feel not rested."

I sat cross-legged on the leather bench and wished for my great old woodbin.

"Wait till tomorrow, Karen," Karl said. "You must be very tired."

"I rest on the train." She looked at me. "Some times."

"I understand," said Karl. "A trip on the train with a youngster running wild – "

"I know it was hard for you, Mama," I said real quick, "to come to the city."

"Yes, Karen," Karl went on as if I wasn't there. "It must be hard to manage the farm practically alone."

"We do just fine at home, Mama, don't we?" I said, quick as scat. I sure wouldn't let Mertie run me down like that. "Even if we have to stand up to the wood-haulers and the neighbors by ourselves."

Mama was turning her head from one to the other as the nasties came.

"Whatever you put up with now," Karl said, "will be well paid in the spring. Half the money I bring home will go for another horse and one or two secondhand implements. The rest will be for you to spend on the house and yourself."

"What we put up with, Mama," I said, getting louder and louder, "is more than money is worth."

"Now see here – " Karl jumped up and came toward me.

"Another beating?" I asked, real smarty.

"Young lady, in all you're life you've never known what discipline is. A few more spankings might – "

"Stop!" Mama stood up from her chair as mad as me and Karl put together.

"I hear nasty words. I hear other nasty words. I will not have two tantrums made from same cloth."

Karl hustled to hug Mama and make up to her and everything, saying he wouldn't argue any more. I came next, careful not to kiss the same cheek of Mama's that Karl had mucked up with his mouth.

Mama started to talk and laugh very fast so we wouldn't get our mad started again. She talked mostly about me, which was all right until she blabbed something about how I was growing out of my baby fat.

"Time flies! Our Corinne will soon be rolling her eyes at the little boys in her class."

That was lots better, even if it was something like Mertie might say.

"Is my little man for home." Mama was glad enough Karl wasn't saying something spiteful any more.

Karl looked straight at me. "But those braids. In the city here, kids just can't wait till they're old enough to cut their hair."

Mama's smile went out with a gasp. She had put a lot of work into my braids just to make me look extra nice for him. How could she do that if a lot of my hair was cut off?

"Out of her baby fat?" He just didn't see what his dumb talk about braids did to Mama, or that I was getting mad, too. "Let me see for myself."

I let him dig his fingers into my shoulder blades to see how I was growing up. But when he went on up my neck and poked just under my head, I jumped up and stomped around the floor.

"There never was any fat around there," I yelled.

If that had been Mertie, I would have smashed him one, and who would blame me?

"Oh, come on," he said, like I'm a little baby. "What did I do?"

I broke into crying and ran to Judd's room. I didn't howl out loud, just dropped on the bed and sniffled the tears out.

Mama came in, soft and slow, and undressed me like I was sick or something. She combed out my braids, too.

"Is all right, your father was teasing to make the fun."

"He told you that, maybe," I spit out. "He as good as called me a little fathead."

Karl's worried face showed outside the partly open door. Mama pushed the door closed.

"Is not so. He does not understand good the girl."

"That makes us even. I can't understand him either."

"Ssst, it is the trouble we find when we grow to the woman," Mama shushed me. I lifted my head and looked at my mother. "He is fine man anyway."

"Mama, that's the first time you ever told me anything about" – I sat up – "about how to grow up."

Mama, her face pink, went out the door. She had said all she was going to.

I huddled on the bed and tried to make a mad picture about Karl.

He spends a lot of money on a plow, which he expects Moses to pull for him. Moses gets mad and makes Karl pull the plow instead, hitting him with a whip if he doesn't.

The picture is so stupid it falls to pieces.

I slipped under the bedclothes and went to sleep.

CHAPTER 21

K-BOY

When I woke up, Karl was gone to work.

I fooled around a while with nothing to do. No Moses, no chickens and not even a woodpile. I told Mama I was going outside.

"Be careful not to get lost," said Mama. "Be careful of the cars. Be careful – "

I walked back and forth on the little roads in front of all the houses. Cars came along the big road between them but not one sleigh.

The houses were big but not such a much, so old-looking and squeezed closer than trees in the bush. All of them smelled like the gas stove I saw in Karl's place. He just started it to make a breathing sound, then lit it with a match. A lot of the houses had a sour smell like beer or home brew and some of them, as I went by, must have had boiled cabbage or garlic inside.

For a while I didn't find anybody, meaning anybody around my size or age. Until I found a boy with a big 'K' knitted into his sweater.

"Hiya, Ken, wait up," I called to him.

"I'm sorry," said the boy. "I seem to have misplaced the name of a charming friend."

I shook my head.

"No," I said. "You don't know me. I came on the train last night."

"Oh? But you called me by name."

"I guessed it from that 'K' on your sweater. A kid at school has 'K's' all over and his name is Ken."

"Remarkable," he grinned. "Mom knitted the 'K' for our last name, Kissel, but it's delightful to be called Ken. My mom is a beautiful knitter, don't you think?"

I nodded.

"I like Kissel for a name. Mine's Corinne Kragh."

"Pardon me for asking, but do you spell both your names with a 'K'?"

I showed him my pendant and told him all about the 'K's' and about Moses and the train and things. Ken told me, almost like bragging, about his dad and mom.

"You're sure lucky to have such great folks, Ken. I have a grand Mama, but that's as far as it goes."

"I'm sorry to hear that," and he was. "I think everybody should have a fine family like mine."

"There aren't such a many good daddies," I told him. "I tried to adopt one, and I know."

"Pardon me," he asked. "But how do you adopt parents?"

"Like, if I wanted to adopt your folks," I said, "then I would come to live with you like your sister."

"But 'adopt' them – " His forehead puzzled up, then he grinned happily.

"Ah, it's clear to me now," he said. "You want a nice family like my mom and dad. Would you care to meet them?"

"How many kids do they have?"

"Only myself. I'm sure it would be delightful were you to join our family. There are so few children in our neighborhood and they are – ayah, look out!"

Two boys about our size or a little bigger ran and stood in front of us.

"Hey, Maggot, lookee," said the one in front of me, with a hard kind of grin. "Kissel dug up a country cousin. Watch this."

He whacked his foot against mine, so quick I hadn't a

chance to save myself. Down I went into a snowbank.

"Great trick," I said, not mad a bit. "You knocked away the foot I was standing on mostly. I want to try that on Mertie."

"They're a pair of toughs, Corinne," Ken yelled. "Run."

Ken should have run himself, but instead he went for my boy, fists flying like a windmill. I just sat in my nice seat in the snow and watched them. Never before had any boy taken my part in a fight. They were more likely to fight me!

Ken's fists whizzed around even if they didn't hit much.

"Nice work, Stinky," said Maggot. "That got this schmoe going."

Maggot took a jump closer to where Ken was trying to fight off Stinky, which wasn't any better than waving his arms. At first I thought Maggot was coming to kick me or pound me while I was down, and I know some things about that. But no, he went to help Stinky beat up poor little Ken.

I rolled to my feet with a hard fist stuck straight out, a trick I learned from fighting with Mertie.

Maggot tried to dodge from me. I changed aim halfway. Maggot threw up his arms, which my fist crashed through like paper. He stopped me with his nose, though, and yelled about it.

Stinky looked around to see what the yell was about and sure looked when he saw me ripping his pal to bits. Four or five of Ken's flying fists got in his face, then he yelled, too.

"Oh, I see," I said, watching the two toughs rubbing their faces. "If anybody yells the fight stops?"

"Did I defeat him?" Ken asked sort of anybody. "How?"

"Can't nobody take a little fun?" Maggot snuffled, feeling his nose.

"I liked it," I told him. "Now let's try a few nifties of mine."

Before I got my fists up, they hustled around the corner talking something about a "hellcat."

"I am so sorry to involve you in this awful brawl," Ken said, all worried. "Did they injure you?"

"You took all the pounding there was from that Stinky – such stupid names."

"Oh, that's their tough names. They make them up themselves."

"They do? I know a kid who's tougher than them, and he hates to be called 'Rabbit'. How about your name?"

"I'm perfectly happy if you call me Ken," he said.

When we got to Ken's house, he opened the door and stood back with a little bow to me. That meant I was supposed to go in ahead of him, but a lot of cold air went in first before I knew that.

The room had one dinky little lamp on the ceiling and the window wasn't such a much either. I could just see a big mussy-looking woman sitting behind a table with her elbows braced on it so she wouldn't tip over into a lot of brown bottles and wet stains. Under her eyebrows her eyes looked black and closed or maybe open.

Some bottles lay around the floor, one of them smashed right into the side of another. Such a sour smell everywhere, but I could see that the Kissels were no bootleggers, just people that bootleggers sell stuff to.

A cot in the corner sagged almost to the floor. On it was something about the shape of the pyramid of Egypt in my schoolbook. This pyramid had a belt buckle on top.

"Dad," Ken walked over and poked it. "Dad, I'd like you to meet Corinne Kragh." The pyramid didn't move, but Ken went on talking, "May she come to stay?"

"Ken," I said, trying to get a better look at the mess lying on the cot. "I'm not a kitten to give away or something."

"I beg your pardon, Corinne," he said. "I just thought how delightful – "

"You see, there's my pendant to think about." I held it for him to look at again. I looked around the whole room.

"A very nice pendant, I'm sure," said Ken. "But I fail to see what is the connection."

"Well," I explained. "Before anybody can talk adopting, I want to know if your dad's name has two 'K's' like yours?"

"Two 'K's', you say? No, his name is George."

"George?" The woman at the table lifted her head off her hands a little but left her elbows ready in case it came down again.

"Sheorge, gimme 'nother one – 'nother one like a good man."

The pyramid stayed where it was, but something else rolled a little on the cot and gave out a groan.

"Too bad, Ken," I said, tucking the pendant away and inching toward the door. "Anybody I adopt has got to have the two 'K's'."

CHAPTER 22

PYRAMID OF EGYPT

The pyramid of Egypt began to roll around a little. A big tousled head came up from somewhere else along the cot. I couldn't see some eyes, but the thick eyelids turned toward Ken, toward me, around to the messy table and to everything else in the room. Then they opened a little and settled back on me.

The head roared, in English maybe, but such a mush-mouth it was I couldn't understand a word.

"I'm sorry for that, Dad," said Ken. "Corinne is very nice, and I thought it would be all right to introduce her."

The man sat up with another roar and swung a fist and arm as big as three hams. Ken went tumbling across the floor like Inez, my cloth doll, the time Mertie hit her with his baseball bat.

A great big man, bigger'n Karl, got off the cot and went all shaky across the floor to where Ken was trying to get back on his feet. Ken wasn't using his left arm to help.

"Run, Ken," I yelled, "or duck – do something."

A hard *whap* landed square across his face, and again Ken tumbled. He lay on the floor with some blood where one of his eyes should be.

"You put his eye out," I screamed. "You're killing him."

The man snarled and staggered again toward Ken. I wasn't afraid for myself; I could always run. But Ken wouldn't run, even when he had the chance.

I aimed myself at that pyramid with my punching arm, back and legs in a straight line the way Karl had showed me how.

Thump!

It was like punching a soggy haystack. Ken's dad was too big and heavy for me to make much of a fight, but he stopped anyway. I stood watching him, all ready to give him another or run or something. He bent over a little and pressed his hand to his mouth, which was twisting around like he was sick.

"Ken, Ken!" I ran and lifted him from the floor. "Ken, we have to get away from here."

Ken's dad seemed to be looking, but he didn't try to stop us.

Ken's mom picked up a bottle by the neck and scolded away all mushy just like Ken's dad. She waved the bottle around, not caring about the stuff running out of it over her arm and the table.

"C'mon, Ken. I'll help you walk." I pulled the arm that wasn't hurt across my shoulders and partly dragged him to the door, watching his dad all the time. When I closed the door behind us, I heard somebody in the house being awfully sick.

The cold air seemed to fix Ken a little so he could stand up by himself. He whimpered a little while I helped him along the street until he could walk by himself. Then he stopped and looked back.

"I must go home," he said.

"I can't let you." I hadn't thought of where to go, except away from that place. Now I knew. "You're coming with me."

Ken still wanted to go back home, but he walked along with me anyway. It was hard getting him up all the stairs, but Mama opened the door for us.

"Oh, the nice boy," said Mama, looking hard at me. "You do this thing to him?"

"Mama, I didn't touch him. He's really hurt."

Karl was home now. He looked at Ken. Mama washed the

blood off Ken's face while Karl eased his sweater off. That was when Ken started to feel the pain.

"No broken bones." Karl pulled the puffy eyelids apart. "His eye seems to be all right, too. Mostly a cut on his cheek." I flopped onto the bench and pressed my face against the cool wall. I shut my eyes, too. My stupid shakies were coming on now that the trouble was over. My head had a whizzing sound inside, and a picture tried to come, a picture of a man as big as the pyramids of Egypt coming at me with a huge club.

"Corinne, Corinne." I didn't hear Karl until he shook my shoulder. "You haven't told us what happened and why you brought this boy here."

Ken was lying on Karl's bed with only a little sniffle once in a while. I felt better, too, after I told Mama and Karl, with a little bit of bawling, about what happened at the Kissel's.

Karl stared up at a corner of the ceiling with a hard look on his face.

Suddenly there was something I just had to say.

"Now I know," I said. "Now I know what a beating is."

"Yes, you certainly should," said Karl.

CHAPTER 23

ME AND KEN

The alarm clock buzzed, then stopped with a click. I heard feet thump on the floor in the dark and shuffle toward me on the bench. A match lit with a bang and in its flare-up Karl reached for the string to light the electric lamp. He bent down and lit the gas stove with the same match. Then he sat on a chair and reached under it for his socks. I remembered the mornings in our log house.

Karl saw me sitting cross-legged on the bench with the blankets wrapped around me.

"Corinne, why aren't you sleeping?" he said.

"I'm watching."

"Watching? Watching for what?"

"I'm watching that Ken is all right."

"Well, is he?"

"He's still there in Judd's room. I heard him sleeping every time I listened at the door."

"Why do you think he might not be there?"

"Well, the Kissels – "

"You mean to say you were watching in case the Kissels came here to get Ken?"

I just nodded.

"Do you think they are as bad as all that?" Karl got his breakfast things out. "I mean, I know George at work and he practically lives for that boy – most of the time, anyway."

"He scares me," I said. My blankets shook. "The look on his face when he . . . you know. And he hit Ken with his fist, his fist, mind you. Ken is only a little kid."

"And you waded into that, fighting?" Karl stirred a bubbling saucepan.

"I had to, I was scared. Not for me because I could always run away from him."

Karl looked hard at me, holding his stirring spoon up in the air.

"You didn't get much sleep last night, did you?"

"Just little bits," I said. I stopped to yawn. "Do you think he will be all right now?"

Karl put the spoon down and turned the fire a little lower so it wouldn't burn his porridge. He seemed to want to get his hands free but then didn't know just what he wanted to do with them.

"About Ken? Yes, he's safe enough now. You get some sleep now."

I dropped on the bench. I let my eyes close though I wasn't asleep, at least not quite. I felt some awfully strong yet awfully gentle hands smooth and tuck the blankets around me. And I felt a little squeeze on my shoulder.

When I woke up, there was Ken. Not that he woke me; I just knew he was there. I peeked out under a corner of my blankets and saw him sitting at the table in a stream of sunshine from the window.

And was he eating! Mama said afterward that she made enough porridge for the three of us, but she kept putting it in Ken's bowl until it was all gone.

His eye was a dark blue for a long way around it. His left arm hung in his lap like he didn't feel like using it though Karl had said it wasn't broken.

Then he saw my blankets wiggling.

"Corinne," he said, standing up anxiously. "Corinne, how are you this morning? Are you all right?"

"Of course I'm all right," I snarled. "Except for sleeping away most of the day."

I sat up on the bench and pulled the blankets tight around me. Karl's room was not cold, but my fancy nightie was like nothing against warm old sleepers.

"But you look – "

"Can I help it how I look?"

I grabbed my pile of clothes and headed for the door, blanket ends trailing. Ken scooted to open the door for me. I yelped at him and scowled him back to his chair.

"Did I do something to make Corinne angry, Mrs. Kragh?"

"You will understand some time, Ken," Mama told him with a chuckle. "This is a girl."

"Ma – ma!" I scolded, and banged the door after me.

I looked at the picture in the looking-glass, an awfully clear and close up one this time.

"Hello, Me," I said to it. "No wonder Ken looks at you like you got two broken legs. Just look at your sick eyes and your hair like a messy crow's nest on top of a tree! I've seen prettier things hopping around in a mud puddle."

I bubbled cold water across my face and combed my hair, holding it in place with my nice rosebud barrette. I held up my dress to look at it, pulled at a wrinkle or two, then put it on.

"Now I'm all fixed up." I stepped away and looked myself up and down, turning around a few times. "Who has to tell anybody now I'm a girl?"

"Good morning, Corinne," said Ken when I came back, the blankets on my arm but still trailing on the floor. "How are you today?"

Ken was looking at me, actually seeing me. At home, where all the kids know me so much, nobody would see me even if I came at them waving a meat axe.

"I'm fine, of course, but how about you?"

Maybe he only wondered where the tough kid was who punched Maggot in the snout and his father.

"Fine, just fine, thank you." He smiled like he was wonderfully happy. He held his left arm like it was sore, his eye wouldn't open more than a bare slit and once he put his hand to his head like he had a headache. "Especially after the lovely breakfast your mom so kindly served me."

That dude was ready to settle for just porridge. Mama broke some eggs into a frying pan in which sausages were already sizzling. I caught Mama's eye and tipped my head. Mama cooked an extra egg and put one on each plate. Mama's plate got one sausage, mine got two and Ken had three. He was polite but hungry and cleared his plate.

"There is other egg in the pan," Mama said.

I said, "Mmp – mmp!"

Ken said, "No, thank you very much. I've had a wonderful repast."

Mama gave him the egg anyway, along with another sausage that happened to be hiding in the pan. That, for breakfast, seemed to be about right for Ken.

When he was finished he said, "Excuse me, ladies," and ducked out to Judd's room.

"Gee, Mama," I whispered. "I remember when I ate last but I don't think Ken is so lucky."

"Tish," said Mama. "The boys do always eat good."

Ken came back trying to get his sweater over his sore arm.

"I am deeply grateful," he told us, his face twisting with pain. "Now I really must go back to my parents."

This doughnut-head was packing up? It made me shiver just to think about where he wanted to go.

"Oh, Mama, he wants to go so soon?" I said. How could I stop him until at least his parents had time to sober up? "What will Karl say?"

"So rude of me," Ken took his sweater off again. "The least I can do is express my gratitude suitably to your parents."

That wasn't what I was thinking about, but if the nut wanted to wait till Karl came home because he would be a meanie if he didn't, well –

What can you do all day with a boy? Ken talked so nice with me and Mama, saying our names twice in everything he said, but we just couldn't get something we could all talk about. With Mertie, I could count on a good fight sooner or later, but with Ken? No – o – o.

"Mama, play us some of that nice stuff on your accordion."

"It is not like home; my fingers cross up on the buttons."

Mama felt shy in front of Ken.

Mama found a checkerboard somewhere. I lost the first game to Ken and threw the checkers on the floor.

"I am sorry," said Ken, crawling around to pick them up. "I did not intend to win."

"I'm not mad at you, just at the stupid checkers."

"You should win this time," Ken said when we started the next game. After a few moves I was winning. Then I caught him sneaking one of his own men off the board.

"Hey, that's cheating," I yelled at him, jumping up and nearly upsetting the board.

"I was only trying to help you win this time."

"That doesn't matter; it's cheating anyway. Now I'm mad at you."

Ken shook his head over me a good many times as I stormed through the day with him.

Karl's feet at last came tramping up the stairs. Checkerboard, books and everything else dropped to the floor as we both ran to meet him.

"I thank you extremely for your kind hospitality," Ken bowed some more. "I regret that I really must return to where I belong."

"Yes, things should be better at your home now," said Karl

looking again at the bruised eye. "I'll come with you."

"No, no," from Ken, suddenly in tears.

"Just to see that you'll be all right," said Karl, his fist clenched though he didn't know that.

"You are angry at my dad, and I don't want to see two such nice people fight."

"Just as you wish," Karl opened his fingers.

"I'll go with you, Ken," I said. "I'm not mad at anybody."

"Better you should not go," said Mama, fearfully pulling me between her knees.

"Mama, we'll be all right, won't we, Ken?" I pulled myself away from her fingers like I was getting loose from bind-weed.

"I'm sure you will be most welcome, Corinne," he said, with one of his stiff low bows, where you can't see his face until he's finished it.

I caught Karl's eye, and he gave me a little tip of the head.

"C'mon, Ken," I said, picking up my coat. "I promise to be nice as pie."

CHAPTER 24

ELEPHANT OF INDIA

We started to Ken's house with hoppity-skips like we were going to a sugar party. The closer we got, the slower we walked, especially me.

When we got there, Ken made me wait down on the walk, where I could run if I wanted. He stood on the top step and pushed a button beside the door.

"Why don't you go right in?" I told him. "It's your own house."

"Thank you, but I must ring – " Ken stopped with a gulp when the door rattled and clicked. He seemed to brace himself for something, his chin up high.

"You came here just for another beating, didn't you?" I scolded.

The tall heavy woman, her eyes open for sure this time, opened the door and grabbed Ken. I balled up my fists in my mittens and came closer.

"My boy, my boy," the woman sort of cried, then held him back when she saw his hurt eye. "My poor boy."

Ken turned a little and bowed. "Mother, I'd like you to meet my best friend, Corinne Kragh."

"H'lo, Mrs. Kissel." Ken's kind of politeness was hard to come up to.

"Do come in, Corinne." She smiled at me like I was something special. Maybe she didn't remember me or anything else from yesterday. "Do I have your name right, dear?"

Ken bowed me in like he had before. I stepped through the door, looking all ways, my hard fists still bagged in my mittens. Ken's mom was nice as pie, but it hadn't been her that I punched in the belt buckle.

The room had the same small light, but it looked brighter. All the bottles, stains and broken glass were gone. So was the sour smell, mostly.

Then I saw *him*. He was in a big cloth chair with places to lay his arms on. The pyramid of Egypt, which must have been made of all the stuff he drank turning to fat right where it dropped, was taking a rest all over his lap. His face was smarter-looking now and a lot like Ken's.

Ken took me over to him.

"Miss Kragh," Mr. Kissel stood up – way up until his head almost shoved through the ceiling. "I'm doubly delighted to see you."

I had to tip my head back to look as high as his face. I tightened my fists even harder though I could see it would be better to scoot out the door if he wanted to get even for that poke I gave him.

Where had I got all that nerve yesterday?

"No, no, Corinne. You have nothing to fear from me," he said, like somebody had told him what I was thinking.

How was Ken doing? Oh, his mom was sitting him on the cot and taking the sleeve off his sore arm.

"I, uh, thought you would be mad at me."

"Because you assaulted me, my dear?" He patted his belt and winced slightly. "Well done, and the best action under the circumstances. It made me ill which diverted my vile humors."

He had little anxious twists in his eyebrows when his eyes turned to where Mrs. Kissel was looking at the bruise on Ken's arm.

"Yes, I saw your gallant rescue," he went on, "though my comprehension was not otherwise at its best."

"Then you mean everything's all right now?"

"Let me put it this way: we are utterly grateful to you for

harboring our beloved son while this outrage," he pointed to the room, "and this," he pointed to himself, "were thoroughly put to rights."

I took off my mittens. I was no more afraid of him now than if he was old Moses. But I still thought Moses was a nicer guy.

"I can't understand why," I said. This might make him mad again, but it was a big question and I just had to ask. "Why did it happen?"

"Why?" It took Mr. Kissel a lot of thinking before he tried to answer. "There is a craving in all of us, you in your way and I in mine, to indulge ourselves occasionally."

"You mean, like some men who once in a while go out and get d – "

"Drunk?"

That made it all right for me to say it, too, " – get drunk and beat up somebody they've been mad at for a long time?"

"I do not hate my son," he blazed. I got set to kick out of my chair and away. "Never have."

"I didn't think so. He's been telling me all the time what a great home and parents he's got," I said. "He deserves the best, don't you think?"

He flopped against the chair back like he got a mighty big slap in the face. He sat there a good minute with eyes closed and his face pulled up like he was hurting.

"Well put, my young philosopher," he said real slow and opened his eyes again.

"What does that mean about you and Ken? You won't hit him any more?"

"Ken?" He looked puzzled.

"You know, over there."

We both looked to where Ken's mom was bending his arm up and down.

"Oh, a fair question, I'd say," Mr. Kissel said. "No doubt

the situation is much like an elephant of India."

I looked at his big heavy tummy. He caught my look and pulled it in a little bit.

"When one of the big beasts becomes crazed and runs amok," he said, "the first one he attacks is his beloved mahout, his closest friend."

"I'm still afraid that Ken, sometime, might – "

"You have a direct mind, young lady." He took my hand in both of his. "By this I make a vow to myself. I hope to heaven I never put myself in a position to break it."

Ken was so nice to me I almost hated to go back to Karl's place. He had great books about the whole world, and he played nice music on a little fiddle that he called a violin.

His mom brought in a big shiny plate with a smaller plate of nice cookies and two fizzling drinks with straws stuck in them.

"Algernon, dear," she said. "Would you care to offer some refreshments to our guest?"

Ken jumped up and took the plate to me with another of those bows. I took a drink off the plate, though I was afraid it might be bootleg stuff. I smelled i,t and it wasn't sour. Then it tasted good, so I knew it was all right.

"Ken," I said. "Where did that new name your mama used come from? You told me your dad's name is George?"

"That's my name – Algernon." His face lost some of its happy. "The boys around here give me a bad time over it."

"Why didn't you tell me?" I sucked some of the sweet drink through the straw. "If you don't like it so much, you could make one for yourself, like Maggot and Stinky did?"

He shuddered all over like a cold draft hit him.

"No, Corinne," he said. "You call me Ken so charmingly I wouldn't think of anything different."

When the cookie plate got empty, and I didn't see Ken eat even one, I put my mittens on, and Ken put my coat on me.

"The trouble with you, Ken," I said when, instead of a simple 'so-long,' he took both my hands and bowed over them. I stopped, trying to think exactly what the trouble was with Ken.

Here was me, mind you, who blew up and quit when I got paddled for the first time. All the other kids I know get lots of that, but do they run around trying to adopt any daddy they can find?

Then Ken, trying to make the best of things while his parents were sober. When they were not, he could get some terrible things, even a beating – a real clubbing kind of beating.

"The trouble is," I told him. "You're such a gentleman I can't understand you."

CHAPTER 25

K FOR CORINNE

By that dinky little light in the Kissel's place, I saw Ken's dad, a bottle in his fingers, leaning against the wall as stiff as a board. Ken's mom sat on the middle of the table with brown bottles in her lap and all around her.

"I'll clean up this mess," I said to Ken, going to pick up the bottles.

"No, I'll do it," Ken said, polite as anything.

"All right, then I'll sweep the floor."

"Here you are, little girl," said Karl's voice, and he handed me a broom.

"Thank you, Daddy," I said and started sweeping.

Karl called me "little girl" now because I adopted Ken's dad so I wasn't a Kragh any more. But why did I call Karl "Daddy" when I never did before?

Ken came by, carrying out some dirty straw.

"They gave me four bruises today," I told him.

"Oh, I did better than that," Ken said. "They chopped my leg off with an axe."

I woke up in a hurry. I was really sitting on the leather bench in Karl's room. Mama had her accordion on her lap, and Karl sat sideways on a chair with his arm on the chair back.

Ken left such a big lonesome after him that nobody knew what to do. Karl asked Mama to get out her accordion. She played so many soft sweet songs that I got somewhere between sleepy and stupid.

"Yes, it is so much for the little girl," Mama said. Then

Karl must have said "little girl," too, just a while before and that's how it got into my dream.

Tonight I wasn't mad any more at Karl for going away to the city or spanking me or anything. I just couldn't talk to him – well, maybe "H'lo" or "Please pass the butter."

I could never again think of anything to talk about or to laugh about or to see what he thought about. Everything like that was switched off just like the electric lamp over our heads when you pull its string.

"Poor old Pokie," I said with a big sigh. "She'll never be there any more to sing and dance for me."

"What about Pokie?" said Karl. "You never told me."

Mama explained, talking in Old Country.

"Never will I make a friend of a chicken again," I said.

"No?" said Karl, not really interested.

"Neither will I make a friend of anybody," I said, mostly for myself. "It's so awful if they might die or go away or something."

Mama and Karl started talking in Old Country, so fast they couldn't hear anyway.

"Ken is so stupid," I said a little louder. I was thinking: how could he make friends with me so big when he knew I wouldn't be here more than a week? What I said was, "How can he say his folks are so great when they get drunk like pigs?"

They talked fast and without holes in it where they could listen even to themselves.

"Mertie, too," I went on talking. "His dad makes the kind of stuff the Kissels get drunk with. When he's busy making it, Mertie has to run out of the house and keep people away. Who's got the worst of it, Ken or Mertie?"

Who would have thought I would be this lonesome for mean old Mertie with his rabbits and fights?

"What do you think?" Karl stopped talking to ask me.

They both waited while I thought about it.

I shook my head, "It's hard to say, but it must be nasty for both of them."

Lots of kids do things that get their dads mad at them. But did Ken, I mean Algernon, go around saying he had no daddy and try to adopt another one?

"I'm much less than a perfect parent, too," said Karl.

My head jumped around so I could look at him. Was he trying to get silly?

Accordion time was over. Mama reached for the pork and beans box, but I took her accordion and packed it in the box.

"It is such the nice child," Mama thanked me.

Nice child? Me? Poor Mama never got mad, never even slapped my fingers. Right now she didn't know how lonesome I was for her even when she was sitting right there.

"You seem to handle a problem very well from what I hear," said Karl. "Maybe those kids are trying to do the same."

"But I never do anything the best way the first time," I said, twisting my arm up behind my back.

"What is it?" Mama asked. "Is it a scratch?"

"Just trying to – oof, trying to feel if have any baby fat."

Karl grinned but didn't say a thing.

No, nothing but muscle there now. Maybe Karl paddled my fat to jelly and it all oogled away. I hurt while I was losing it, maybe, but who wants to live all her life inside some baby fat?

"Not Me," I said out loud, but Karl was talking with Mama in Old Country again.

In his city clothes Karl looked so different from when he walked through the bush holding me on Moses' back or when he tossed me above his head after we danced our two-sizes kind of kicking polka. He talked different, too – not the fun and teasing way we used to talk to each other. I didn't understand him any more.

Would Mr. Avard really be such a much if he was my daddy? Or Mr. Henshaw or Cubby's dad? Like Mama said, even a fine man could be hard to understand.

Then there was Mr. Kissel – hey, didn't I blab to Ken about how to adopt daddies? I told him then that I don't want Karl any more. What if Ken came and adopted Karl?

I tippy-toed across the floor real slow. Great. Without any pyramid of Egypt in the way, I had lots of lap to sit on and dangle my legs. A big arm was right there to wrap myself in. The arm curled tighter and was it ever warmer than some dusty old scarf!

Karl and Mama were talking so hard that everything I started to say was smashed into by a bundle of Old Country words.

At last, after Karl got mixed up and told me in Old Country how to sell the firewood and told Mama in English to quit wiggling so much on his lap, Mama smiled and stopped talking.

"Well," said Karl, "you have something to say?"

Yes, I certainly did but it was so hard to start.

Plok, my good old pendant fell out right into Karl's hand.

"What's this?"

"Oh, my pendant!" I snatched it and laid it on my hand. Here was a great chance to explain what I was hurting to say. I peeked up at him past my eyebrows. Yes, I had his attention.

"See these two 'K's'?"

He nodded.

"Well, that supposed to be for us, all of us."

"But there are not enough 'K's,' eh?" said Karl, fingering the pendant. "Is that what you're saying?"

"Let me tell it," I said. I had thought I could explain what I needed to around that pendant. I meant that when Karl was gone to the city it felt like a 'K' was taken off my pendant.

"If I get what you're driving at," Karl said, "let me tell you that's your pendant, and you don't need another."

"No, no, no!" I stopped him. I didn't mean to ask for another pendant.

Karl looked at me, probably at the tiny tear I couldn't hold back. His mouth opened as if to say something more, then closed again. I saw it stretch into a teasing grin like the old Karl.

"Very clever," he said. "But don't you know you can use letters as many times as you like? Just go back again to the first one and you have three of them. Lots enough to make Karen, Karl and you, Karenne."

"Oh, crazy!" I said. I could have swatted him like a bug. He had messed up my picture so much I just tucked my pendant back where it belonged. Now I didn't know how to tell him what I started.

"Speaking of letters," he pressed a big finger on the tip of my nose and wiggled it. "Who has never sent me even one letter?"

"Well, now!" It was my turn to tease if I could. "I just can't remember getting a letter from you."

"Come now! What about all the letters I send to Mama?" he scolded.

This was no time to tell him I wouldn't listen to what was in them. Mama gave up trying to read them to me.

"Well, I might, starting from when I get home – " I said, but I couldn't finish. Karl grabbed me by the armpits and tossed me over his head in those big hands, like he used to after our dances.

Watch yourself, Me, I told myself. You're a big girl now so don't go kicking your legs in the air like a baby. I put on a stony face, too, though I giggled through it.

"All right, I promise, I promise, I promise," I yelled.

The way he looked up at me was so great it almost hurt.

"What do you promise if I let you down?"

"A big fight if you don't," I threatened, sticking my tongue out at him.

"My two childs," Mama laughed happily.

He made no move to let me down.

"Well, I might dance with you if Mama plays her accordion. But how can I when I'm stuck up here?"

"A little better," he said. "It won't get you down, though."

I knew what he wanted. I used to throw my pudgy arms around his neck and slobber a kiss on his face before he would let me down. Baby stuff, and I didn't have a scrap of baby fat left.

"I'll kick like old Moses."

"That never worked either."

When you get adopted, Betty Fanson said, you find that nothing and nobody is like you knew before, not even yourself. You have to start all new.

"Don't you think," I took a deep breath, a real big one, and spoke seriously. "Don't you think I am getting too big for this sort of thing – Daddy?"

"What?" He let me slide down his arms like I used to off a haystack. Mama's eyes rolled, and her head rolled though she said nothing. I would have tumbled to the floor if I hadn't wrapped my arms around his neck.

"What did you call me?" Karl asked, completely flabbergasted.

"Oh, I forgot to tell you," I said. "I'm calling you 'Daddy,' Daddy."

"Since when?" I think he liked it the old way, like we were two kids playing together.

My arms hugged him tighter.

"Since I adopted you – just now."

About the Author

Cecil Freeman Beeler was born in 1915 in Nokomis, Saskatchewan. He grew up on a farm during the Great Depression, and his roles as a child were determined by the ebb and flow of prairie seasons. From an early age he worked as a wood-hauler in the winter, plowman in the summer and grain-hauler in the autumn. As a young man, he joined the air force and later moved to Winnipeg to begin a technical career. In 1980, he retired to devote his time to writing. Today, he fills up his retirement years writing stories for young adults. Still gripped by memories of his youth and a resourceful young girl he knew at the time, Cecil Freeman Beeler portrays Corinne Kragh's adventures against the backdrop of life, as he knew it, on a small farm on the Canadian prairies.

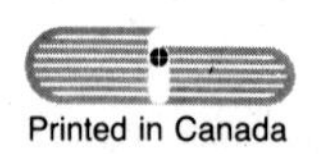

Printed in Canada